JOHN TOFT

THE WEDGE

D1785388

W. H. ALLEN
A division of Howard & Wyndham Ltd
1972

© John Toft, 1972

Printed and bound in Great Britain
by Butler & Tanner Ltd, Frome, Somerset,
for the publishers W. H. Allen & Co. Ltd,
43 Essex Street, London WC2R 3JG

ISBN 0 491 00861 9

**LONDON
BOROUGH OF
REDBRIDGE**

N

acc. no.

81/544

class no.

GHERS

017292371

PS. 1138

FOREWORD

What's the point of an introduction? For the reader it's only an annoying block that stops him going straight into the story. For the author, anything that does this is a menace to all the work he has put into the book.

I believe that words are precious, and that not too many of them should be wasted on an introduction. Yet there is a point to this one because it seems to me that John Toft is an unusual writer in that he brings up a sharply-seen world in a single paragraph—social, physical, historical. If words in a novel can't do this, and maintain it all through whatever plot the author blesses it with, then the novel might just as well not have been written.

People in *The Wedge* exist. It is surprising how many people in novels do not. Often they live vividly only for the writer, and fall emptily onto the paper, flattened by preconceived psychoanalytical data that has nothing to do with a flesh-and-blood human being.

The two main people in this novel, Ernie and Sheila, escape such a fate. With all their faults and rough glamour they are exceedingly real people whose horizons in early life extend step by step, in perfect time with the rate at which they can develop. They want to do the right thing by themselves and others, a hazardous exercise because they also have a desire to 'get on'. Ernie knows how to, but Sheila doesn't. As it happens, neither of them succeed, because that is not the point of their lives. Everything is more complicated than that.

Ernie, who never becomes 'Ernest', is the pillar of the book. When he goes through the throes of a WEA summer school at Oxford we see the experience through his eyes alone. Consequently it is full of social and humorous nuances, and the value he gets out of it was not quite that which society hoped he would get.

Sheila's long affair with Malcolm, the young bargee is, to my mind, a romantic set-piece that manages to maintain its realistic impartiality, and so forms the backbone of the book.

The barge and canal scenes, and the life Malcolm shares at a derelict cottage with Old Vincent, who still suffers from being gassed in the Great War, are memorable. Malcolm brings out one vein of Sheila's love, but it turns into the strongest of her life. As a sort of anchor to reality, however, she cannot escape the benign influence of Ernie.

This is a rich book, well written, without superfluities. For a beautifully sustained tale of ancient and modern love in an English Midlands setting I can think of none better.

ALAN SILLITOE
Wittersham

I

Ernie loped beside Sheila in his grease-creased raincoat that had been somebody else's before it became his. As his grandma was always saying, almost with satisfaction, there had to be sacrifices for his High schooling. He was, Sheila thought, a walking sacrifice from his scalpy Vaselined hair to his taut boots with their brassy eye-holes. Cycle-clips kept his trouser bottoms out of the February slush, and his ankles looked like Mickey Mouse's.

She's got her eye on my boots again, he thought. As if they summed him up. The boots were like they were because they had got to last, not because he had chosen them. A working girl now, she had some nice things, that blue coat and spotted scarf. She wore long stockings, bought jars of make-up and sometimes borrowed her mother's tongs. She smoked, too, as if she had done it all her life. She was well-made, everybody said. He felt empty, as usual, thinking how beautiful she was. But what did it mean to him? He had known her too long for it to matter. He wanted to think they need not bother about appearances. Or about talking even. But he ached for her to say something. They had shared everything once, moving like twin fishes. Now it was as if he watched her from where they had been, and it was cold. She loved going to the roller-skating rink and once he went and saw her zooming round, sealed off in her joy. It was the same when she went walking the town, on the look-out

1

for lads. She pinched their handkerchiefs out of their Sunday breast-pockets and they had to chase her giggling through the streets or into the park. He was excited, seeing her. But she never snatched *his* handkerchief.

When she met him, Sundays, he was always on his way to or from church, being the assistant organist now. She laughed—he was just like some sad grey whippet—and pointed him out to her new companions. It frightened her how differently she saw him now. He was repulsive and had once been her best friend.

She squelched the ridges of grey slush, splashing her stockings.

'Careful,' he said, drawing her to drier streaks of the pavements.

That was him all over, careful. She smirked in the shop-window lights, but he seemed not to notice, staring ahead.

Why does she smile like that? He turned his face to the lit church-clock. They were on time, no thanks to her. She seemed to take longer and longer getting ready. Did she have to make her face up so sharply when they were visiting Mr. Davies, who wouldn't like it at all? It was her own business, he tried to think, but he felt responsible for her and—it seemed silly—for Mr. Davies too. He wished he hadn't brought her. When he was not with her he longed for the time when he would be; when it came he lived in a different suspense and relaxed only when they separated again.

She noticed his glances at the clock. Was it really necessary for him to be short-sighted into the bargain? He'll be like a middle-aged man by the time he's twenty. He was part of all that hemmed her in: chimneys, grave- ›
yards, gas-lamps, all that was out of date, enduring and

2

dismal. He was like the lank squinting house of the music master whose coloured glass front door he now tapped lightly, afraid of cracking a panel. He shuffled his boots, deferential, expectant. Sheila tossed her head back, hands deep in her pockets.

Miss Davies had one leg shorter than the other and wore a built-up boot. Her feet were like Ernie's in a way: humble feet. Sheila wanted to tread all over them and crunch the toes. She feared the strength of her own feelings. Gladys had a quiet voice; her face and body were good at fading into backgrounds. Ernie hovered like a spirit on tenterhooks waiting to be judged. Gladys took them to the kitchen where two pairs of old slippers stood warming by the fire.

'Your feet'll be that wet, I'm sure. You'll catch cold if you don't change. Come on now. Your shoes'll be dry for when you go. Don't be shy, Sheila.'

'I'd rather keep me own shoes on, thanks very much.'

She only wants me to do it, so as I shan't tread black on the carpets.

'I'm sure Ernie's going to be sensible, aren't you?'

He had already been sensible and stood self-conscious in the shapeless slippers. Typical, Sheila thought, pulling her face in the darkness of the passage. The music room was where Mr. Davies and his spinster daughter did their living—if, Sheila thought, you could call it that. Portraits and busts of the great composers watched like warders from every wall above squads of leather-bound books and scores. The crimson blankety bobble-edged curtains smelt of the sooty outside damp. A baby grand and a gramophone with an old-fashioned listening horn looked like a couple of Victorian great-aunts, one deaf and the other grinning with huge false teeth. The little

Welshman flirted up from his hide chair. He had been strict with Ernie and rapped his knuckles in the early days but he was fond of him, too. Gladys managed to give the boy a sense of fellow-feeling that reassured him and opened up abysses.

Why are they kind to me, he wondered. They want to make you one of themselves, Sheila would have replied. You *are* one of them.

She hated the way the music master's jugular veins —or whatever they were—clenched among the dry flaps of his neck, reaching down his collar like sticks. But she was troubled by the Celtic eyes deep behind their gold-rimmed glasses.

'So we meet Ernie's Sheila again.' He produced his well-known growl-and-twinkle and said to himself, I thought as much: pretty now and cheeky. There was a raw flash beneath his guises of father, musician and church-warden. Sheila glittered.

'Well, I'm Sheila, anyway—a bit older now.'

'So you're a big girl, eh?'

Mr. Davies said exactly the same old things as everybody else but made them sound tremendous.

'Don't stand around dithering and looking silly, Gladys. Go and make the tea. Come and get yourselves warm. You're in charge of the crumpets, Ernie.'

Ernie took the curly brass fork as if it were a baton. Smiling, Gladys jerked away to the kitchen. I shan't sympathise, Sheila said to herself, I'm not going to help with the tea. Instead, she sank down in Mr. Davies's chair.

That's the way to be, Gladys murmured as she boiled the kettle. Sheila's got the right idea.

Mr. Davies fidgeted on a chair he wasn't used to, talking hard to avoid studying the girl's pose and dissatisfied mouth.

'So, Ernest, how's your grandfather?'

Everybody had a feeling of something crucial. Coming in with the dumb waiter, Gladys poised to hear the reply:

'Still very poorly.'

Ernie did not want to speak about his grandad. It seemed he was always doomed to be pitied by people and that wasn't what he wanted at all. They seemed not to think he had any power of his own. Sheila brightly said just what he dreaded her saying:

'It'd be terrible if he had to give up the idea of going to college, wouldn't it, Mr. Davies?'

'Indeed it would.'

I just don't want Grandad to die, that's all, Ernie ached to say, but he peered stonily into the fire and tried to keep his breathing quiet.

'Why don't you put a record on the gram., Dad, whilst I bring the tea in?' Gladys was one who filled awkward gaps and answered prayers.

Ernie loved listening to the gramophone: it was a relief sometimes not to have to make the music. Sheila groaned inside. She knew exactly what sort of music it was going to be.

'How'd you like that, Sheila?' Mr. Davies beamed.

She half-shrugged and nodded.

'Very nice, I daresay.'

'*Oh for the Wings*. Will that suit you?'

'I'm not fussy.' She swung her bob of hair, maliciously innocent.

Ernie had already extracted the record from the cabinet with irritating familiarity. Mr. Davies put it on

5

and the famous treble rose above the hiss. The Welshman sat back thrilled, his dark eyes shut, and heard his childhood in the song. He could ignore the cheeky girl who made him feel old and randy. But his eyes blinked open now and then and flashed on her a look without time or place in it, startling her thoughts, which were so often about men, but not ones like Mr. Davies. All that the song meant to her was Ernie's white world of dismal goodness, surplices and stagnant holy water, scraped scalps and organ pipes. Mr. Davies' glance made her feel like something lurid amidst such things. She shuddered, but with pleasure, at the thought of her future. Then in the doorway came Gladys, who seemed to Sheila to have no future, habitual tears in her grey lined eyes at the soaring of the song.

'Well, now, what do you think of that, Sheila?' Mr. Davies spoke as though the spell had been of his own working. Gladys slipped back to the kitchen. Ernie smiled, as did Sheila, but her smile was not so happy and she said nothing until:

'You can't beat a boy when he's really good,' Mr. Davies observed.

'It's a bit too good, though.'

'I don't know what you mean.' Mr. Davies's eyes did not speak quite so definitely as his voice.

'Well, you know, goody-goody.'

Ernie's happy smile faded.

'Ernie sang a bit like that, didn't he—before his voice started breaking?'

'Yes, it's a pity boys' voices have to break just when they're at their peak.'

'Ooh, no, it's a good job they do. They'd make funny men if they didn't.'

6

She smirked fully at him, right into his face, and almost guessed how much he wanted her to go on.

'How about another record?' Ernie intervened.

'I think we should let Sheila choose this time.'

It was Gladys again, always on hand like a duster to bring shine and smoothness back.

'Oh, you wouldn't have any of the stuff I like, don't worry.'

'What sort of *stuff*?'

Sheila shrugged.

'Well, my favourite at present is *I get a kick out of you*.'

Ernie blushed.

'Father's not very keen on that sort of thing—it's not his generation. I like it though.' Gladys smiled a bit too sweetly for Sheila.

'That's putting it mildly, Gladys. I think that stuff's the beginning of the end.'

Sheila looked as though she didn't understand but half did.

'It's what these brazen monkeys jigger about to.'

That means me, Sheila thought.

'I love dancing, and I'm going tonight as a matter of fact.' She turned the last bit on Ernie.

Gladys applied a light laugh like ointment.

Her father grunted and sighed and put a favourite bit of Brahms on the gramophone. But the girl's long legs crossed and uncrossed irritably in front of him till he felt himself lured and lost in that slippery future which he wanted to control and could not. This time he heard his death in the music. Though Gladys and Ernie and even, in spite of herself, Sheila were moved by it, they did not know what he knew. Troubled, they

7

gazed at his lidded, fastened face. Gladys slipped from the room, just as her father's eyes opened on her impersonally. Ernie was trying hard to set his mind on analysing the music, which darkened Sheila with the past and a world not of her kind, in which a few people thought themselves everybody and everybody else nobody. Ernie perhaps thought he was getting into that world, but he was nobody really.

There were crumpets and cream-cakes for tea. Sheila kept quiet and ate like mad until she belched loudly and blushed because everybody looked and she had to say 'pardon'. Then she wanted to go to the lavatory but dared not ask in case they thought she wanted to do more than pee.

After tea the entertainment continued, and got worse. Mr. Davies asked Ernie to accompany Gladys 'in song'.

'Oh, but, Dad, there's the dishes to be washed.'

Don't look at *me*, Sheila thought, eyes averted.

'Please, Miss Davies.' Ernie had his shining dog look. 'She's got ever such a good voice, Sheila. She should have been a professional.'

'Why aren't you, then?' Sheila asked, more suspiciously than she had intended.

There was a little pause.

'Obvious, isn't it?' Mr. Davies sounded sandy-throated. Gladys lifted her crippled leg and gave an apologetic smile. Sheila's stomach cringed. Ernie looked sadly at her. Christ, she thought, what have I gone and said now?

'I'm that self-conscious,' Gladys said. 'Or was when I was young. My voice wouldn't seem to come out right when I had to sing in public.'

'Did you ever try?'

'Only once really.'

8

'You should've tried again.'

'The once was enough.' Mr. Davies ended the talk and Ernie slid into the opening of a Schubert song. Sheila was sweating by now and sniffed furtively at her armpits. She squirmed and goose-pimpled as Gladys entered the song with terrific fervour and swelled to its climax. Her voice was firm and sweet, but she and Ernie put so much into the performance that they looked like comedians on a silent film. Mr. Davies applauded with massive hand-smacks and Sheila felt obliged to give a few flips herself. And then there was somebody's cradle song in which Gladys rocked an invisible baby while Ernie minced, owl-eyed, at the keys. The music master rumbled a kind of descant and Sheila was taken with a fit of giggles, because he lifted his glasses up his head and fluttered his eye-lids in time with his obligato. Sheila sat and spluttered into her handkerchief, finally letting go and, as she said later, practically peeing herself, at which the song stopped dead and they all looked at her. She gave a round of maniacal applause and started up, hating them.

'I shall have to be going now. Just look at the time.'

'But——' Ernie began.

'I'm going dancing tonight. I told you before, I've got to get ready, haven't I? We only came for tea, didn't we? You can stay on if you like. Thanks ever so much for the eats, Miss Davies. Ta-ra, Mr. Davies.'

Something made her use words which she knew would grate on the Welshman. As she hurried from the room, she heard him telling Ernie to stay where he was. She wrenched into her coat and stood at the door to be let out. Gladys came jerking up.

'You go dancing a lot, I suppose?'

9

'Of course. What else is there to do?'

'It must be lovely.'

'Well, at least there's a bit of go in it.'

'Doesn't Ernie ever come with you?'

'*Him?* No fear. He's too busy with his music and his studying. He's a bit of a bookworm, you know.'

With the accent on *worm* she would have liked to add.

'I thought you were old friends.'

'Yes, but we're different now. We're growing up. Only he doesn't seem to realise. Our ways don't suit each other any more.'

Gladys nodded, opening the door. Sheila breathed the outside air with relief. She wanted to rush away shouting. But she said thankyou and stepped into the wet street. She hurried to where the town's lights glossed the melted snow. She wished she were somewhere where there were more lights and everything was bigger and there was a lot going on. Here the buildings were squat and dirty, with no life in them. She longed for sky-scrapers and signs blazing round every corner. In the dance-hall she could believe for a while that she was among them.

Mr. Davies had gone to fill the coal-scuttle. Out in the dark smell and glint of slack, he somehow wished the girl had not gone, and he felt the front of his trousers. Then he stiffened his neck and shoulders, surprised at himself.

Ernie was staring into the grate. It was like it always was: he was relieved at her going, but there was nothing worthwhile now that she was not there. Why should she mean so much? She never wanted to go anywhere or do anything with him. Why should he bother? But there would be a gap without her and nobody else could fill it. Certainly not Liddy, the only other girl he knew well; she was like a sister to him, now that she had been living with him and his grandparents ever since her mother died. She was everybody's notion of a good girl, and this was why Ernie was never excited by her.

'What a pretty girl Sheila's getting.' Gladys came in and caught Ernie's brooding look. He nodded.

'Not very polite, though.' Mr. Davies set the hod down, glancing down at his flies. 'Still they're all the same today.' Ernie nodded again.

'Oh, Dad, for goodness' sake!' Gladys's tone startled her father and he looked wonderingly round at her. When he had put the coal on, he brushed his fingers together, took out his wallet and handed two tickets to Ernie.

'For the Hallé concert. Take Sheila. Perhaps you'll convert her—to something decent—after all.' The music master glanced again, almost nervously, at his daughter.

II

Liddy loved Sunday. She came into her own with it and felt most herself. Her auburn hair and freckled face warmed with its mild hopefulness. She wore her Salvation Army uniform and felt that life was meaningful. When her mother committed suicide and her brother was put in a home for mental defectives, she had been relieved but empty and did not like to become somebody else's burden. It was hardly possible for Ernie's grandma to make her feel one, since she lay so lightly on those around her. But she was an extra mouth to feed, on Grandpa's pension, so she was glad when the time came to leave school and go out to work. She did not show her gladness as Sheila had done, shouting 'Whoopee!' and dashing home without a glance behind. Nor had she Sheila's 'big ideas'. Sheila vowed never to work in a pot-bank, but Liddy was happy to learn the quick strokes of underglaze painting and how to take care of her little set of brushes. She was clever, too, at dress-making and, with her mother's one useful relic, a sewing-machine, ran things up for Mrs. Hordell and Clive as well as for herself.

On the whole she was glad now for Clive to be in the asylum. It had been hard for him at first, and so for her, but as he got used to it, he seemed to want nothing else. Everybody was kind to him because, save in his fits, he was comical and loving. One thing depressed her: that, seeing him only once or twice a week, she began to notice

12

his ugliness. As a child, she had always been surprised when other people recoiled from him. Now she saw why and disliked herself for her detachment. But that was another good part of Sunday: she visited him and took him toffees and whatever clothes she had bought or made for him. Self-conscious in her outfit, she took the hospital bus into the country, an acknowledged figure on it now. Every time it dipped over the canal bridge she remembered the trips with Sheila and Ernie to the strange hut of the boatees, and wondered where in the world they could be now. They were never mentioned by her and Ernie, but the memory of that day, when her mother had met the barge-man and was later caught in bed with him, hovered in the air about them. Nobody ever knew how much they dared talk of the past with Liddy. And she did not know how far she dared think of it: poverty, sex, suicide, her mother's whole life and death. She was very close, people said. She gave neither encouragement nor discouragement, her standards seeming higher than most and more fully applied.

The red asylum tower came into view, no longer frightening, and the red bus drew up beneath it. She was always the first visitor to reach the wards. People made way for her. She thought that one day she would like to work in a hospital. The well-polished lino, cream walls and smell of cabbage appealed to her as a background to duty. Nor was she put off by tales of maniacs slinging their bed-pan contents over the nurses or chasing each other with axes, bloodshot eyes stuck out on nerve-ends. She saw herself soothing and curing, slipping the axe from the lunatic's fingers and laying his head on her shoulder to cry himself to sleep. Then she smiled at her own vanity.

Through the ward windows she saw a spur of wood-land that overlooked the canal. That was where she took Clive for walks. Once they had found a wild strawberry and he had kept it till it became a bit of green fur.

He was growing faster than ever, one of the largest inmates now. He lumbered towards her, smiling with tiny eyes, among all the other large, lumbering, smiling tiny-eyed others, never children and always children. They romped forward like resurrections of extinct animals got up in human clothes, happy to be on show. A warder directed visitors and visited to seats indiscriminately, as if they were all simpletons. But he winked at Liddy. Clive stepped carefully across the shafts of pale sunlight. Liddy caught his hand and drew him to a bench under the window-sill. Fat hyacinth buds half-opened blue eyes to the light, and Clive's little yellow eyes squinted curiously into theirs, then smiled into Liddy's. He prised her hands open to see what she had brought him. Nut toffee and a pair of boots. He stroked and smelt them.

'These are for when we go out. Shall we go in a minute or two?'

'Oh, aah.' He could just maybe recall the Sunday before, but going out was always a new joy, even though it was what they always did. Everything they did they did over and over again, like seeing how far the flowers had grown in their pots. Year in, year out, he never got tired of these repetitions, and because he didn't neither would she. She knelt and pushed the boots on to his big pungent feet, wondering why cretins had to have other defects as well as mental ones. He stretched his legs into the boots, listening for the leather's creak, and patted his big loose thighs. He grinned up at the girl and

14

noticed her face turned to watch a tabby-cat that was strolling across the shining floor as if it were inspecting the visitors. Clive's hands jerked forward and grabbed the cat round its tender-webbed belly. It scratched at him and pulled his skin but he dragged it single-mindedly into his arms and flopped it on Liddy's lap. It clawed through her skirt and writhed back to the floor, sleeking away under a bench where it began to lick itself fiercely as if it had been contaminated, its pupils clenched to lines. Clive was for grabbing it again, but Liddy held back.

'No, duck, let it be. It doesn't want mauling to death.'

As she leant forward she felt a wet prick of blood on her thigh, like the pang of her brother's place in her life. It was time they went for their walk. The room, quiet at first, now that the inmates had made their first adjustments, grew full of gobbling sounds, lurchings and slitherings which seemed to strengthen the smells. She got the warder to fetch Clive's coat and scarf and they set off down the drive to a path between railway and canal. She stopped for a moment to muffle his scarf round his ears and tug his collar up.

He waved his hands in their grey gloves, as if to challenge the cold to get through her knitting. He ran on for a bit, then waited for her to catch him up and ran again. Then he took her hand and made her run, and it was like running with a clothed pig. He wore short trousers still, and his blotchy raw legs reminded her of her mother's when she let them burn before the fire.

'Cisma t'ee.' He stopped with a cry, pointing to the black firs with their last scufts of snow.

'That's right, love. Shall you be glad when it's Christmas again?'

He seemed lost looking at the tree awhile. She wondered what colour and light he saw dazily there. Perhaps he knew, as she did not, what the robin meant by its glittering stare when it paused with its squat little head on one side looking at his squat big head. He turned to her with a strange smile as if he were going to tell her what he had heard, but,

'Edbes,' was all he murmured and

'Yes,' she agreed softly, 'Robin Redbreast.'

He gave one slow nod of his head, and the bird sped on.

They made for their usual spot, the old wooden bridge across the cut. A path wound half-muddily and half-frozenly down to it, but when they got there they could not get across. The bridge had been smashed at one end and now was just a torn twist of planks, the orange-white inner wood bared in jagged painful points to mid-air.

'Oh, whatever have they done?' Liddy was more troubled than she could say. Clive looked in sad wonder. 'Who could've done it now?'

Whoever it was, they had put an end to one of the fondest habits in the life of Liddy and Clive. They did not know what to do. The girl's eyes fixed glassily on a tangle of briars that hung down like dead worms into the winter stream. Clive sensed despair in her stillness, for he grunted and turned and began careering back up the path, shouting,

'Co' o', co' o'!'

He let his snot dribble into his mouth. He turned round in his running to see if she was behind him. He slipped and fell down thump. He began to yell. His fat and looseness always saved him from hurt, but she had

to kneel beside him in the slush. First she kissed his wet and snotty face because he pulled at her bonnet saying,
　'Ma' it be'er,'
and when she had made it better she lifted him with all her might. She wiped his eyes and nose, glad that nobody had seen them on the ground together and angry with herself for thinking how unsavoury he was to kiss. She glanced at her wet wrinkled stockings and dirtied coat-tail. *He* doesn't suffer really, she thought, it's just me that does and I have to bear it by myself. She squared herself inside her uniform, re-did her bonnet tightly and looked hard into the featureless blueness of the sky. Then, scolding herself, she found that Clive's trouser-seat was wetter than her knees. He tried to look too at the black patch on the wide-stretched flannel, his neck wrenching and his feet shuffling round and round. He touched it with light fingers as if his bottom were separate from him, and he grinned. Oh the little duck, Liddy thought and then smiled: he was a lot bigger than she was now.

　'We'd better get back. We don't want you catching cold.'

　He shook his head and took her hand, and they walked quickly back to the asylum.

III

It was Liddy who went to the concert with Ernie and he was surprised by her pleasure in it. He even began to take a bit more interest in what she did with herself, though he looked on the Salvation Army as a joke. He could not see what she got from it. But the old black Sunday market-place became alive for her when the Salvationists' strong voices challenged the Communists' across the cobbles and the divided gawpers. It was possible then to feel at one with everybody, as the flickering lamp-light brightened the faces of those who went into pubs or came out of churches.

Ernie was a regular among the latter. Once or twice he saw Sheila dressed to kill, on the way to a date or out to catch whatever eyes might be worth catching. Her own eyes glinted ironically at his.

'I can never get over your Liddy joining Sally's Army. However can she wear that rig-out? Honestly, that poke-bonnet on her head——'

'Liddy looks O.K. to me.'

Sheila was lighting a cigarette and studying his eyes for the signs of distaste. Her first puff swirled against his glasses.

'I expect she does to *you*, love. I say, d'you know where they get together, all in their caps and bloody bonnets? Oops, forgot it was Sunday! That rusty tin hut top a Market Street. I bet there're some ronk goings-on there.'

He hated the word 'ronk'. She laughed as he turned

away to gaze over the square at the cold green west in the sky. He longed to make himself so remote that he would not have to go through the feelings she roused in him, feelings he couldn't put names to.

'Allo, Sheila.' Liddy came up smiling in the fearful way Sheila brought out in her. 'You've caught me good and proper. Just out of church, Ernie?'

She knew he was. Their exchanges were nearly always flat.

'When're you going to take me? He's promised to let me hear him on the organ, but nothing's come of it yet. D'you like the organ, Sheila?'

Sheila made a face and looked sarcastically around her.

'No, I'd sooner have the trumpet.'

She had noticed a strapping cornet-player watching them from the band. When he saw her looking, he began to move towards them. Liddy noticed the switch of Sheila's eyes.

'That's Arthur—Arthur Boot. You know, Ernie, I was telling you about him. He's been ever so good to me.'

'Would you believe it?' Sheila muttered.

Ernie frowned, watching Sheila size up the newcomer, who was dark and had a sketchy Ramon Navarro moustache.

'We could hear your trumpet above everybody's,' Sheila giggled. 'Couldn't we, Ernie? You must have powerful lungs.'

'Well, I can give a good puff even if it doesn't always come out as intended.'

'Uniform suits you. Only, I don't think the women's is very flattering.' Sheila gave Liddy a quick down-up look. 'Do you?'

19

Ernie could have hit her.

'Liddy looks nice in it.' He glared through his glasses.

'Oh, yes, it suits Liddy.'

'Ever thought of joining yourself?' Arthur grinned.

'What me? I'm not the religious type. I'm a naughty girl. You ask Ernie. Anyway I don't believe in God any more.'

She surveyed them all, feeling very smart.

'P'raps that's because you've never really known Him.'

'No, can't say as I've had the honour.'

'You should come to the Citadel one night.'

'Is that where he hangs out? No, thanks. I don't want to give up any of me pleasures.'

She dropped her butt-end down a convenient grid. Ernie listened mournfully for the faint sizzle.

'And what are they?'

'What d'you think? Skating, dancing——'

'Courting?'

'On and off. But don't let's go into details.'

They laughed together. Liddy and Ernie looked left out.

'Where d'you go dancing?'

'Majestic.'

'I've been there a time or two.'

'Don't tell me as you dance—you a Salvationist——'

'Oh we don't object to a bit of fun, do we, Liddy?'

Liddy shook her head uncertainly. Ernie gazed and gazed into the darkening sky, his hands clenched.

'So when'll you be going to the Majestic again?'

'Wednesday.'

'P'raps I'll see you there.'

'P'raps you will.'

Sheila and Arthur fixed each other with glinty smiles.

Ernie and Liddy looked at them, then at each other, then away into space. The Army band stood watching the scene as if it were spot-lit, but at last they struck up impatiently. Arthur jerked round, back on earth with a bump.

'That didn't take you long,' Ernie couldn't help grating as he walked Sheila home.

'Mind your own business.'

'Don't you care about Liddy's feelings?'

'She can look after herself. Besides, she's after you, not him. Anybody can see that. Didn't you notice? She wants to come and listen to your old organ. Be careful, duck, else her'll p'raps want to have a go on it.'

Her peal of giggles sent him scurrying home, where Grandma and Grandad were listening to the wireless he had bought them out of money he had saved from playing for weddings and funerals.

IV

Grandad had his bed downstairs now so that he could be in on everything that was going. He was weak and in pain from something the doctor would not or could not name, though nearly everybody else whispered 'cancer'. Grandma heaved up and went and punched his pillows for him while he sat tremblingly away from them. Then she smoothed his head back and her dog, Spot, shoved its nose into his white fingers which hung like shrivelled roots. A fungus-smell wafted up whenever he moved.

'Want your pobs now, Dadda?'

He nodded ever so faintly with a small grey smile.

Grandma padded to the pantry and then to the scullery to get his bread and milk supper. Ernie said,

'Shall I read to you a bit?' and the man nodded again with his embery smile. The boy turned the wireless off and began reading from the Bible at the place marked by a pressed bluebell.

'Now these are the children of the province that went out of captivity, of those which had been carried away, whom Nebuchadnezzar, the King of Babylon had carried away. . . .'

Whatever did he make of it, the youth wondered, stuttering over the interminable names. But Grandad was happy with it: Ezra was where he was up to in his umpteenth voyage through the testaments, and he never missed a chapter and always noticed when any of his readers skipped a bit. He nodded familiarly and murmured some of the names with Ernie: Nehemiah,

22

Mordecai and Mispar. He knew the numbers of the children of Parosh and Arah and Pahath-moab and most of the roll-call that the boy laboured nasally over, clearing his throat, adjusting his spectacles and glancing at the dog who seemed to be listening too and trembled his tail when he was looked at. He was glad when Grandma brought the pobs and he was released to go and look after the rabbits and birds he had promised his grandad to take care of for the rest of their lives. He hadn't bargained for the way they went on breeding beyond all control so that it seemed his caring would last his own lifetime as well.

'Are thee owreet?' Grandad asked when he went back indoors.

'All right, yes.'

Grandad slopped at his bread and milk with little gasps of satisfaction and effort, his thin hands faltering the spoon at his mouth and sometimes missing aim. Grandma wiped his bristly chin at intervals and surreptitiously turned away to wipe her eyes with the same cloth. Ernie could not bear this as he thought the cloth must be infected. He wanted to hit her and at the same time he wanted to hold her flat grey head to him. But he sat quite still and expressionless.

'Stop werritting over them animals,' the woman murmured to her husband. 'They'll manage.'

But he wasn't worrying, only thinking faraway. When he had enough to eat, he lay back and looked at Ernie with hollowly-smiling eyes. Grandma put the dish with its remnants down for the dog and the old man's hands strayed to its petally ears. Now Spot'll get cancer, Ernie thought involuntarily.

In Ernie the old man saw his dead daughter and beyond her the years he had spent working at Selham,

23

the great estate outside the city, the old Earl's place. The family was gone and the estate was a pleasure-park now, with speed-boats on the lake and a miniature railway through the woods, and he had not been there for many a long day. But it was the place where he had been most alive and real and he had begun dying when it was sold after the War and he had come to the town. Now he felt himself going back along the rose-wreathed paths, through the trees where deer peeped at him, to the many-windowed sandstone mansion, whose colonnades spread like arms to draw him in. He was a boy, poaching and pelting from the keepers like a fox, and panting to himself that he would become Head Keeper here one day. His father had thrashed him because he had to go before the old Earl, but the latter merely laughed and pushed them out of his leathery smoky study. A few weeks later the boy was summoned to join the Earl as beater on a duck-shoot. He wouldn't have minded God being a humorous paunchy landowner who would depend on him and fetch him from his bed into the cold mist to muted woofs of retrievers, their noses and eyes glistening like the cobwebbed dew, sharp smells of woods and gardens spurring them on. In September they would drive in the brake, miles towards Derbyshire, to where the grouse-moors sprung with heather and harebells, and they would eat slabs of pie and drink ale from tin mugs and exchange confidences over their smokes. There had been no need for ideas about class-war then than there would be with God, none of that piffle his son-in-law had talked just before he went away and got killed in the trenches. But of course Joe was from this different, then distant and still oh so miserable world of the towns. So it was just what you would expect. And now he had got to give Ernie those—what did Joe call them, essays? The time had come. Joe had written them for his evening classes, being so keen on bettering himself.

The old man raised himself and looked anxiously at Ernie, but the boy soothed him back on the pillows. Such writings they were, filled with destructiveness. But Lizzie had made him promise, they were all she had of Joe to hand on. How would he face her with the promise not kept? He raised his fingers like bits of straw and his wife bent her grey-twined head down to his mouth. He whispered with a soft rattle to her.

'Yes,' she nodded. 'There now, dunna fret.'

She would see to it, she would know what to do. He saw her then as she had been, slim like Lizzie, dark and bronzed among peonies, smelling of fresh hay. He was wafting back, free, into his only world, its days like fields and flower-beds, alive with petal-eyes which opened around him as he floated.

A pan was nudged under the old man and he made an obedient effort. The gas bracket above him was shaded, but his eyes fought through to his bright early life. The woman came to look into his eyes and wondered to herself if this was it, they seemed so piercing, but not into anything that was there. She guessed where he was: Why can't I join him? Why do we have to go on our own when we go, after we've spent a lifetime together? It dunna bear thinking about. But what would *he* do with me not there?

She glanced round at her grandson and their eyes met. He's only a lad yet and hardly so much of a lad as he ought be at his age. He'd be that helpless. He's so half-soaked he dunna know whether he's coming or going half the time.

She turned back to the faraway man.

'Eeh, if I could only see what he's seeing now. Sssh, lad, he'll be asleep in a tick.'

'It isn't me who spoke,' Ernie hissed back.

The old man's bright eyes felt their way round every corner of the yellow room, fluttering for escape which they found, not in any life that had been shared with the transfixed deep-breathing old woman, but further than that, further even than his poaching boyhood, in a sun-lit patch of Selham woods. It was there that once, for the first time in his life, he had been, or felt he was, lost. Nobody was with him. He had wandered out of the cottage while his mam was strewing the hedges with washing. He heard the flapping of huge sheets and saw her bent to her basket, a brown blown figure on the endless green.

He had gone to look for a squirrel, or to gather weathercocks, or just to see what there was to see. He seemed on his tiny legs to be the smallest thing there was in the tall black-green forest where the sun came in blue-gold stripes across fir-branches. He had run a bit on the needle-sprung earth and had ridden logs as smooth as pony-backs and run on again. Down miles away he suddenly saw a wide glistening thing that pierced him like his inward hurt. It must have been the lake but he did not know. He was frightened and stopped. He cried with the longing to bury his face against his mother's skirt and shut out the scaring gleam. He knew that he was lost in an unknown place. It was silent. No bird, even, sang. All there was was the creaking and rustling and soft dropping of vegetation. Edged with that painful radiance, the forest was everywhere, and he was on his own in it.

26

V

'It's all happened before.'

Sheila stood at her bedroom window, having taken the day off from work, not because of the funeral but just because she felt like it. Her mother said that was the way to lose jobs, and it was, but Sheila always managed to fall on her feet, as Mrs. Hordell was fond of pointing out.

In the street below, people were stepping out of their houses to watch Mr. Hordell's funeral. They bent and turned against the March wind that thrust round every corner at them and sent dustbin lids flying to make a knell of their own, hollow and random-rhythmed.

Pinafores furled up against faces. Children anchored on their mothers' arms or on each other. Men, their shoulders huddled into their mufflers and their caps pinching tight at their eye-brows, tick-tocked on their heels and hissed in their breath: they would only take their hands out of their pockets to twist their finger-nails round butt-ends in their drained lips. Then when the hearse drew up they deftly dowsed the fags and stowed them somewhere safe or held them unseen in their palms to be dragged at furtively in the less awesome intervals. When the undertaker's men jumped from the car, their bowler hats lifted straight off and spun like twin jacks down the pavement. Everybody wanted to laugh and nobody dared. They nudged each other.

Liddy came out in her uniform and got into the car.

Mrs. Hordell's veil flew like a crow round her head. Somehow Spot got out and ran barking joyfully through the shocked street, cocking his leg up at every drain-pipe. Mrs. Hordell gesticulated with her handbag, its fake ruby fasteners glinting across the air. Ernie rushed out, wild, in his long navy gaberdine and drove the dog back indoors. It made one last defiant squirt on the shoe-scraper and tripped one of the undertaker's men as they came out with the light coffin. The wind whistled his swearing into nothingness.

Sheila turned away in guilty giggles. It was too typical for words. She looked down again. It was as if Ernie had heard her laughter, for he stood now gaping up at her window, as he often did. Their eyes met and she dared not move. She set her face. It haunted him even more than the box holding his grandad's small remnant. He climbed into the car and the old man now made his last way out of the town he hated back home to Selham, to the churchyard outside its gates.

'It's all right for *him*,' the widow was thinking as wintry grey faces peered at her. 'He's not got any more worrying to do.'

It was to be hoped he could not see through his coffin cracks, for every alteration in the scene on the way to Selham told of the extinction of his past, of his being. The dual carriageway flanked by streamlined semis, the flashing board that said *Selham Pleasure Gardens—the Beauty Spot of the Midlands,* petrol stations and refreshment rooms and public conveniences, all were nails in the unprotesting box. Only sturdy short wild daffodils just coming up by the pathway to the church told of the happy long-gone life and, at the tower's foot, primroses crouched low in their leaves, ready to draw back into the earth again at any moment, just as the old man had been ever since he had left these parts.

At her window long after the procession had left, Sheila felt her sadness shift dimly into triumph. Something made her glad to see the last of the old things and to see her former friend losing so much. It satisfied her that the end of a phase was being marked, that nothing could be the same as it had been. The times she had gone in and out of that house. She knew its every inch, had her own knock on its door, her own way of jumping its two white steps. But some while had passed since she had been in there and she didn't really want to go in any more. Ernie's look had reached her heart out nearly, but it was only pity, she said to herself, flattening a blister in the lino beneath her feet, and she was angry that she still felt for him, that he still preoccupied her mind, even though he looked as dreary as a rained-on chimney-stack.

VI

'What have you got?' Ernie asked.

'Jam.'

'Mine're banana. Change you a piece.'

'No thanks.'

'Why not?'

'I don't want.'

'Why?'

'I just don't.'

There was silence, save for the moaning of the wind.

'Aren't you going to change me a piece then?'

'What have I told you?'

Though she had thought herself rid of him at last, here she was at his side again, traipsing round dank countryside: his Easter hike he called it. Still, she shrugged to herself, what else is there to do on flaming Good Friday?

The wind chucked fistfuls of hail into their faces. Sensible people were at home eating hot cross buns by the fireside while they stumbled across wild shelterless moors. Look at him, *look at him*, in his hefty boots, a ruck-sack on his arching back, his eyes fixed on the grey earth, set on his eternal endurance test. Admittedly, the ruck-sack contained her own food-packet, but he had mainly brought it to carry his bottle of pop. *Pop.* She laughed into her coat-collar.

What must people think of me, she wondered, seeing me with him? But there was nobody about to see at all.

He told her the wireless had not forecast rain. He trotted out the information as if saying his tables. He always trusted authorities. But there it was, the rain, a smoke on the hills, and it made the day sharper to hear his voice, the trees more stark, the hills more dreary.

'We ought to go back,' she said.

'Oh no. The rain'll not be much. They never said it would rain at all, so it won't be much.'

She tagged after him, wrapping her coat well round her and occasionally waggling her bottom just to relieve the monotony and as a kind of mockery of him. Once he peered round at her, suspiciously.

'What're you doing?'

'Nowt.' She hummed and craned her neck round. When he turned forward again, she licked her tongue out and put her fingers round her eyes in the likeness of his glasses.

They were in sight of the hills he loved and never stopped talking about. As Sheila watched them, hostilely, they retreated into black mist. The earth began to smell like old school-books in damp cupboards.

'We'd best shelter,' she called.

'What?'

'*Shelter.*'

'No.'

'There's a church over there.' She came cunningly to him. This would get him: he was daft about churches.

'Where?'

He could hardly see it, for it looked, along with tumble-down farm buildings, no more than an outcrop of rock from the crackled moor. He dashed towards it.

'Soon changed your mind, I see.'

Inside was nearly as bleak as outside. Sheila felt

31

trapped in mushroom smells and folding wafted cob-webs, lice-crumbled pews, greening brass and peeled patched walls. Ernie dropped immediately to pray and she felt further shut off. Good Friday was very real to him. He had already been to Communion, long before she was up that morning. He forced himself to feel appropriate sorrow, but he was too conscious of the girl hovering uncomfortably over him, studying his familiar alien body. What was it he prayed to? That which gave him the groove down his neck, his dim eyes and his narrow shanks?

When he got up, he aired further information, this time about styles of architecture and possible dates. Bloody know-all, she muttered into the wormy pulpit and then glanced anxiously at the altar.

A tiny northern chapel looked fit to burst with a stupendous alabaster tomb. Stretched with his wife, their identical children ranged stiff with ruffs and hard at cold prayer, lay a Jacobean nobleman. Touching these slabs brought home to Ernie the gulf separating the quick from the dead, and that between present and past. But, thinking of his grandad, sealed off somewhere, he felt himself becoming a part of this past, dead like the effigies and already left miles behind down the centuries, faraway from Sheila who was so utterly in her time. The tomb gave him a sense of being a stone in an arch, the feeling habitual to his grandparents though they did not need to know or say it. Sheila poked distastefully at the frozen hands and faces, hypnotised by the un-changing eyes. Sudden fear of their shifting, of the mouths opening with cavernous voices, the fingers crack-ing and dragging her to their death, made her call,

'Oh come on, Ernie, for Pete's sake. It's horrible here.

I'd rather be in the rain. You really are a morbid bug—er—thing.'

She ran out, half-hoping he would not follow. Of course he was right behind her. The daylight was grimmer than before.

'It's going to pour down buckets and that's a fact,' she said.

They wound swiftly down to the dale. Water rushed everywhere, looping the winter-boned hills, joining and leaving the river that fell through shrouds of green, blue and grey, over white-worn limestone and pebbles and deep into the earth again. There were few others afoot and those there were were hardy sloggers safe in oilskins and gum-boots. Nobody had come like Sheila in just a raincoat and light shoes.

They got half-way through the valley and he was gazing at a spire of rock through webs of birch when the rain became a deluge. And they hadn't even eaten their sandwiches. She looked at him, and horribly smiled.

'We'd better make for Thor's cave.' He dared not meet her look. He donned his cycling cape and when it was over his back and his ruck-sack he looked like an ostrich.

'We can eat our sandwiches in there anyway. Then p'raps it'll have given over.'

'P'raps.'

She followed him, tittering at his fantastic shape.

They were wet when they got under the green-veined vault. Others had irritatingly had the same idea. Sheila wanted the place to herself. Two teacher-like women, press-studded and Eton-cropped, dealt out tea to each other from a shiny crinkly flask, adding the milk carefully from a separate container. Their considerateness for each other and disregard of all else made Sheila glower at them. She longed for a hot drink: the thought of pop made her very irritable. Besides, staring at the rain, hands in pockets, a bald man suddenly shot up from the ledge he was sitting on and said,

'Don't want piles up me flue.'

The teachery women glanced sharply at him. One put her sandwich back in its neat holder; the other consulted a fob watch whose tick could be heard all round the vast, slimy space. They prepared to move on, carefully pulling up each other's collars and tucking each other's hair into their hoods. Sheila's face twisted in suppressed fury. Then three boy-scouts came splashing in, all giggles. They watched people's mouthfuls of food and made echoing belches. Sheila could stand it no more. She turned on Ernie who stood there nothing but a streak of suffering.

'I'm going to climb the hill,' she suddenly declared. 'Coming?'

'You can't go out in this lot.'

'I am doing.'

He just twitched.

'Oh well, I prefer to go by myself.'

She was away before he could say a word, leaping up the hillside among the heavy rain-drops, sliding on stones and tugging at tufts of old grass. She got to a hollow sheltered against the wind, and crouched there, not able to sit for the wet. She ate her sandwiches now, taut with discomfort but also stirred inside herself watching the rain slant over the landscape. Clouds loaded over dark farm-houses and bundled across the foaming river. There were sheep standing nearby, all

34

in winter rags, grubby, idiotic and helpless. Ernie-like, she thought.

But she began to feel something grand in the whole endurance of everything around her and was almost glad to have the rain dripping through her hair, down her forehead, soaking her shoulders and seeping up through her shoes. A broken black tree creaked beside her and she felt its protest as her own. She was reminded of the boat-lad, Judder, when they had met long ago on the cut: it seemed like a dream now. He was the sort who would stride and kick out when necessary. Somewhere in the distance, blotted out now but there, surely, not far away, were his hills, the Roches, whose ruggedness she liked to think he shared. She felt hollow and outside herself.

And then Ernie dashed up with his worrying common sense.

'I've got Liddy's sou'wester here.'

'Well, I don't bloody want it now.'

'Go on.'

'No.'

'Go on.'

'Oh, well.'

'Have my cape as well.

'No thanks. *You* need it.'

He gazed at her through his splashed spectacles, but she did not notice his appeal, only his absurdity. She flounced off down the hill-slope and made her way further along the valley.

He ran up behind her, shouting,

'We'd best go back the way we've come. It's shorter and more sheltered.'

'I hate going back. I came to see the whole way and I will see it.'

35

'But you haven't got the map.'

'Give it here, then.'

They both knew she wouldn't have a clue how to read it.

'All right, come on. Only don't blame me if we get drowned.'

'I'm drownded, as it is.'

Drownded, he thought. How she still talks.

He had to run to keep up with her.

'Mind that puddle.'

She put her foot straight into it. The water squelched out from all round the top of her shoe as she walked on, pretending not to care. It was his fault for calling out. She was worn out and wanted to be at home. Why was it so many miles away and why, oh why, were they here at all?

Ernie felt at that moment how hard it was to be human, to have a tired clumsy body crushing the earth and toiling in the mud, to have to endure this solid separateness from things instead of entering into them as a spirit might.

'There's a bus at six,' he said. 'I reckon that if——'

'I'm tired of hearing about your reckonings.'

'What's up?'

'Nothing—you would never understand.'

'Yes, I would.'

'Doesn't matter.'

'It does to me.'

'Well, if you really want to know, you make me sick.'

He paled.

Oh God, I've done it again. She softened.

'Tell you what—let's try thumbing a lift.'

'I suppose there's no harm in trying.'

'Whose thumb?'

36

'It'd better be mine as I'm——' He was going to say 'a man' but dreaded a sarcastic come-back.

'Get on with it then. You've let one car go past already with your dithering.'

His thumb was useless. Drivers just grinned or stared stonily at their soddenness. So Sheila lifted her skirt up, for the hell of it.

'Don't, Sheila. Stoppit.'

'Oh, for God's sake——'

A lorry shuddered and stopped a few yards past them.

'Yippee!' The girl snatched off her borrowed sou'-wester and made a dash, hearing him call.

'It won't be long before the bus comes now.'

He was balanced on one foot like a peewit.

'Well, wait for the bloody bus then. I'm off.'

She didn't want him to follow her, but there he was again, climbing after her into the hot oily cab.

'Will you be going far?' The young driver moved his jacket for them to sit down.

They steamed, squeezed down together. Sheila sat in the middle, the gears at her knees.

'Just Leek.' She looked at him and went slightly shy. 'Sorry we're so wet.'

'That's O.K. It's a change to be having company for the long journey.'

'You've got a big load on,' she said. Ernie sat clenched, still hearing the tone of her voice when she had said he made her sick.

The driver spat out of the window.

'I dare say you long distance drivers get lonely, don't you?'

'There's compensations. No knowing what you might pick up on the way—like now for instance.'

'And I suppose there's a certain something to being alone on the open road.'

'Yes. It brings out the tinker in me.'

They laughed, their heads nodding together. Ernie sat mute, his stomach somehow cringed up.

'What's your name?'

'Paddy.'

'You're Irish.'

'From Liverpool. Everybody's Irish there.'

She told him their names though he hadn't asked.

'And how old would you be? Eighteen is it?'

'Yes.'

'Seventeen and a bit,' Ernie at last chimed in.

'Then you've got the best part of life to come. Don't be wishing it away.'

'Has the best part gone for you then?' She grinned round at him.

'Christ, no!'

'I thought as much. You're not that much older than us. Are you?'

'Just that much as makes all the difference.'

'Oh, yes, I'm sure.'

'What a pity now——'

'What's a pity?'

'You're not old enough for us to stop and have a drink together. The Mermaid'll be just coming up.'

'You're working. You aren't allowed to stop at pubs, are you?'

'I do what I like.'

'So do I.' She twisted round at Ernie. 'We'll come with you.'

'Don't be so daft,' Ernie muttered. 'We'll miss the bus.'

38

Sheila wanted to hit him.

'Oh shut up.'

Patrick looked surprised and pleased.

'All right, but *I'm* not coming.'

'Well thank God for that.'

He sat seething in his place while Pat lifted Sheila from the cab and steered her to the pub.

'I'll have a port and lemon,' she said airily at the door, thinking that was the thing.

'Oho, will you then?'

'I just want something warm.' She sounded small and uncertain. He felt sorry for her, seeing how young she was.

'Whisky and hot water will do you nicely.'

'Yes.'

She was disappointed to find the pub nearly empty. Her couldn't-care-less walk went unnoticed in the low lamp-lit room. She didn't think much of the place, it was so old-fashioned, with sawdust on the floor and worn knotted benches for seats.

Still, there was a blazing fire and a burnt yeasty smell that steamed from two old women who were sitting at it and plunging hot pokers in their ale. The two ancient heads turned Sheila's way for a minute and then bent together over their sizzling. Three old men played skittles and spat, and twinkled as if in the know. Pat came up with the drinks.

'Ey, just a mo.'

She fished in her pocket. 'I should have paid—in return for the lift.'

'Get away with you. I'll not be paid for by a school-girl.'

'Schoolgirl? Me? That's an insult. Look, please let me pay.'

39

'Say no more else I'll get me temper up.'

'Your paddy, oh yes. That'd be worth seeing.'

They looked gleamingly at each other, seeking but not daring to find hidden meanings.

'What shall we talk about?'

'You could tell me your life-story.'

'It'd be all lies; there's no point.'

Lies can sometimes say more than the truth.' She said this importantly as she had read it in a magazine.

'Now who's being Irish?'

He studied her intently. She gave what she hoped was an enigmatic smile. But *he* was the enigma.

'D'you think your four-eyed friend will still be there when we go back? Maybe he'll hop on a bus.'

'We can only hope,' she murmured, then in a flash of fear added, 'No, he'll be there. He won't leave me.'

'He's a bit of a nuisance to you?'

She shrugged but something in her was glad that Ernie would still be there.

'Suppose we stay here an hour or two?'

He was having her on but she did not see.

'We can't do that.'

'Why not then?'

'We've got to get back home.'

'Why? Why don't you come to Liverpool with me? I'd bring you back tomorrow.'

'Ooh, don't be so daft.'

Why was it daft, though, when it seemed to be just what she wanted? They did such things in films. She wanted to do something, anything so long as it wasn't humdrum. She would never be the same again. Ernie would have a fit. She yearned to go to Liverpool in the warm lorry, through the night, sitting by the handsome driver. Then perhaps to sleep in his arms? She gazed into the fire and the whole room glowed around her. The more she thought about possibilities, the more handsome he became in her mind. But then she blinked and looked at him again and was disappointed to see a boiled complexion and the low moist set of his eyes.

'Come on.' He nudged her with his knee.

'My clothes have dried on me. I don't want to catch cold. . . . All right, I'll come.'

She hardly knew she had said it. He looked so strangely at her.

Then the bar-door opened hesitantly and Ernie peeped in, a flush in his otherwise ghostly features. He blinked around, tip-toed forward and then stopped under the publican's slow scrutiny. Then he scurried to Sheila and Paddy, watched by everybody now.

'Are you coming? The bus'll be here any minute.'

For answer Sheila looked at the Irishman, who curled his lip at the youth and then slowly drained his last third of Guinness. He slapped his mug on the table, silently rose and led the way out into the now softened rain. The bus-lamps came, piercing the chill blackness. Ernie dashed out, a hailing silhouette, splashing in invisible puddles and calling,

'Come on, Sheila. Thanks for the lift, Mr.—er—Paddy.'

Sheila heard the man spit from the side of his mouth into the darkness. She shouted,

'Liverpool, here we come!'

Ernie already had one foot on the bus-step. He craned back to hear what was going on. The girl lightly touched the Irishman's sleeve, but he drew away and his voice sounded afraid and very Liverpudlian.

41

'I was only pulling your leg in there. I was just trying you on. You're only a kid—I mean—I'm a married man, love.'

He pushed her towards the bus. She hardly saw night-time land or sky, or Ernie or Paddy, only bleak vacancy. She mounted the bus automatically and Ernie tugged her down beside him.

'What was all that about?'

She looked blankly at him, then

'I wanted him to take me Liverpool,' she said.

His eyes goggled.

'You what?'

'I asked him to take me Liverpool. He was going to at first. Then he got scared.'

Ernie's mouth opened but no sounds came out. She turned away, beginning to smile. Paddy's lorry was just overtaking the bus. She caught a glimpse of his silhouette slipping away. She kept her head to the window and shook with laughter. Ernie felt her shudders through his arm.

VII

Climbing from the side-car of Arthur Boot's motor-bike, Liddy smoothed her green velvet jacket and white dress. She glanced non-committally at the Majestic Ballroom's windows from which music and chatter scraped the black air. Arthur's heart sank as he parked his bike. He lit a miniature cigar to give himself confidence and kept squaring his chin into his neck. Liddy wondered what exactly he expected of her. She felt vaguely that, whatever it was, it would be beyond her to give. She did not care much for dances. They often seemed to be an excuse or rehearsal for something else that was never mentioned outright. Each couple moved around wrapped in some private dream. Liddy had to keep pushing Arthur's hands up from her bottom. She wondered how he would react if she suddenly slipped her hands round his bottom in the middle of a quickstep.

By the time Arthur had had a few frozen dances with her, he was so fed up he wanted to head for the snooker saloon. She was in one of her many mousey moods, far-away and half-baked, answering questions in words of one syllable, as if they had only just met; she danced, as if doing physical jerks to a higher command than any his fingers or feet could give.

He steered her to the buffet where he cheered up almost too obviously at finding her friend, Sheila, laughing and flirting. Sheila looked up superciliously at him, as she imagined Joan Crawford might have done.

43

'Allo, allo, allo,' he trumpeted. 'Look who's here.'

His glance went all over her thin red blouse and she half turned her face away. He looked common out of uniform: his neck grew thick and raw from his creased collar and his forehead was greasy. He was broad-bottomed and loud. Yet there was something, too, that made her want to challenge him.

'You've got Liddy into your sinful ways, I see.'

'Not all of them, I'm sorry to say. And dancing's not a sin, you know.'

'Depends how you do it.'

'Depends on your partner, you mean.' He winked at Liddy, but Liddy knew the wink was not really meant for her. She couldn't stand banter.

'Mmm.' Sheila looked understanding.

'Liddy's quite safe with me, aren't you, love? She's *always* safe.'

'Oh, well, the night's young yet.' Sheila smiled.

'Don't you think *you'd* be safe, then?'

'With you?'

He nodded and smirked.

'It depends.'

'Want to try me out?' he asked.

Sheila shrugged, giving a sidelong look.

'Can do—if Liddy doesn't mind.'

'Oh, no, I don't mind.'

Arthur bought Liddy an ice-cream soda and a packet of crisps and took off eagerly with Sheila.

'I was looking for you,' he said, 'from the start. I hoped you'd be around.'

Cat-like she smiled.

'Well, I do come here often, like I told you, so there's no need to ask me *that* question.'

44

He wasn't at all bad to dance with: firm, and just the right touch of roughness.

Liddy sank into a chair, thinking to herself, let him go and good riddance. But no, she relented, it's not him, it's me, it's my fault. She gazed round the high hall with its balls of light which seemed to move with the glittering colours of the unbearable clash of the music. She wondered what in the world she was doing here, stilled amid this swirling, and she studied with a kind of fear the preoccupied faces of the dancers. They were so strange and impersonal, their bodies dressed up so carefully and expectantly. They were willing their tiny instants of romance to come true, dots of light that grew faint in the workaday days and years.

'Liddy's so buttoned up,' Arthur whispered as they fox-trotted past her. 'She just never lets herself go.'

Sheila glanced across at her friend, who sat nibbling her crisps and looking so plainly out of place. She ought to have been back home with Ernie. They were made for each other, surely. Drab. If I flirt with Arthur Boot, it'll do her no harm. But do I really want him? Good God, no. But she let his hands slide round her, despising him for his slobbery absorption in her.

'You don't seem to be enjoying yourself much, Lid,' she said, affecting sympathy, when they returned to the bar.

'Oh I am—it's just that I prefer watching.'

'That doesn't say much for my dancing, I must say,' Arthur over-heartily laughed.

'How about trying mine, then?' Sheila asked, her eyes a-glitter. She snatched Liddy's hand. Arthur grinned, mesmerised by the two girls.

'Oh, no,' Liddy cringed back, feeling menaced.

45

But Sheila dragged her on to the floor as Arthur stood swaying with mirth. I'll soon show *him*, Sheila thought. It gave her a thrill to take the man's steps. She loosened Liddy's tautness more deftly than Arthur could ever hope to do, and she manipulated her into the mould of the dance as if she were throwing a pot. And Liddy had to confess, when breathlessly they rejoined the youth, that she had enjoyed herself no end. Her eyes were bright with fearful admiration of her friend, and his turned jealous and mistrustful. It was Liddy who longed to go again, though she dared not say so: it was lovely to twizz in the mass of twizzing, stepping in and out under the flashing domes, feeling the gusts of skirts, touching bodies, to the glint and tinkle of bangles, parting and touching again.

On the sideline Arthur gaped at the uncanny grace and intimacy of the two girls as if they were snakes curling together. He wondered why he was never able to make Liddy so alive. He didn't realise that he couldn't make Sheila so alive either. This life he saw deepened his longing for her. When she flashed her self-intent smile at him now and then, he wanted to dash to the lavatory and get rid of the ache there and then, in case she whistled away from him before the evening was over. But she didn't. From that time she dominated everything around her, dancing with Liddy and Arthur alternately, never letting them have a go together. When Arthur bought them drinks while Liddy was away in the ladies' powdering her sweat off, Sheila egged him on to lace her American soda with gin. Though he could hardly bear the waste of money, he did as he was told, so that in the final dances Liddy, her eyes gliding all over, sagged and lolled like a rag-doll in Sheila's grip.

46

When the time came for going home, Arthur offered Sheila a lift.

'Where'd you prefer sitting—pillion or sidecar?'

'Pillion, of course.'

'Oh, no,' Liddy cried. 'There's a bit of a drizzle starting. I'll go pillion.'

'No, you won't duck. You'll be safer tucked up inside in *your* state.'

Liddy certainly felt very dizzy, so they laughingly arranged themselves. Arthur wrapped his leathery coat round Sheila while Liddy squeezed into the sidecar. Sheila linked her arms round the youth's stomach and, putting her head on his broad back, said, as he revved up,

'Go real fast, fast as you can.'

He did, and she felt in this too that the power was really all hers, passing through Arthur to the machine and snatching them through space endlessly. She savoured the roar and the blasting smell. From time to time she caught a glimpse of Liddy's face by lamplight, tense and protesting silently through the sidecar top. She was the one who suffered most as they careered round cobbly corners, sheered the curbs and grooved the tramlines. Sheila was reminded of the Waltzers at the Wakes and didn't want the ride to end.

When it did, Liddy gave a stifled thankyou and goodnight and dashed home, about to fetch up the crisps and soda. Sheila and Arthur were left chortling, elated. They wandered up the back alley in the blackness. Through the quiet they heard the Hordells' kitchen door open. A torch shone down the yard. There were tripping steps and then the sound of Liddy vomiting in the lavatory. Arthur and Sheila fell against each other helpless with

47

huddled giggles. He took his opportunity and got her in his brawny arms.

'Not now,' she said.

'When then?'

'Sssh. She'll hear us.'

They listened till Liddy had gone back indoors. Sheila wished she could see Arthur's face to know whether she fancied him or not. She felt his large chest against her raised elbow and then his thigh closed into her and she let him kiss her. He could hardly believe his luck in starting out with Liddy and ending up like this. He had expected the evening to be a wash-out. He drew back and felt musingly at his privates through his trouser pocket. He wondered what the girl would do if he plonked his cock suddenly smack in her hand. She's a queer fish, though, he thought. You have to work ever so carefully yet you wouldn't think it to look at her. She's spiky but terrific.

'You're terrific,' he whispered.

She tittered. 'I know.'

'Why did you have to keep dancing with Liddy, though?'

'I liked it. I'd like to be a man.'

'What would you do if you were?'

'I'd just go free around everywhere. I'd never get tied down. I'd see the world. I'd have a good time and not care.'

She made him feel somehow uncomfortable. It didn't seem natural to him for a girl to be like this.

'Do you care now?'

'A girl has to, doesn't she? She might get in trouble else.'

He cursed inwardly. He knew he would never get her.

Except by force maybe. He put his hand on her neck and smoothed her like a cat.

'Jet,' he called softly, the word coming to him from nowhere. 'Jet.'

She twisted out of his moist touch.

'Think I'm a cat or something?'

She felt she was in a film and must act accordingly.

'Got a fag?' she lightly asked.

He scratched a moment's light on their faces. She did not really care for what she saw of his. Two smouldering spots of nothingness moved about their broken muted talk and they breathed each other's smoke. Until suddenly he bent on her harshly.

'Eyup!' she cried and raised her fag to singe his ear.

He yelled, grabbed her wrist and made her drop the cigarette and lunged into her.

'No you don't,' she yelled. 'Geroff!'

Ernie was at that moment returning from a nightly stroll with Spot. He hesitated before running towards the shouts. Then with an awful sense of draining he entered the alley and shone his torch on Arthur's behind and up into Sheila's wild face.

'Send him off, Spot.'

But the dog just went and wagged round the writhing couple. So Ernie pulled at Arthur's coat while Sheila took the chance to go dashing home in a fit of giggles. Arthur knocked Ernie flying through a gateway. His torch and his glasses smashed on a step and he had to feel his way around. Arthur, finding that his trouser seat had split, took himself off, and his motor-bike was soon heard popping and blasting through the town.

Liddy, who had been trying to vomit once more in the lavatory, had heard the scuffling and, taking up a brush, ran down the yard to see what was up. She stopped dead when she heard Ernie's familiar voice muttering,

'Oh God, where are they?'

She thought he had gone mad. She ran to help him. He just managed to choke a shriek as she touched him.

'Whatever's the matter?'

'Is that you, Liddy? Where's Sheila gone? There was a man trying to get her. Has she gone home?'

Liddy's heart sank with she hardly knew what depression. She was not jealous at all, only disgusted.

'I bet she egged him on,' she murmured, putting her foot on Spot's lead, 'I bet she did.'

VIII

Grandad was the ground of Ernie's life, there to the end and then ever after. For the first time a death made him feel that a part of him was elsewhere and he was moving towards it. The paraphernalia which spilled out of two Gladstone bags—a silver horseshoe, locks of hair, snaps and studio photos, a ring, a lady's glove, ribboned letters and deeds—bestrewed the mothballed bedroom like clues on a chase which, taking the path out of time, would lead straight to where the old man sat nodding and smiling and saying,

'Whatever kept thee so long?'

But there was one set of objects which did not belong to Grandad, and Ernie grew goose-pimply as he handled them. There was just a book and a bundle of writings, all there was, apart from himself, to show that his father had ever been on earth. Though his mother too had died at his birth, Ernie felt he knew her from the Hordells' loving talk of her. But his father had been less than a shadow, for they knew so little of their son-in-law and they told Ernie even less, merely that Joe had courted and married their Lizzie in a matter of months and then gone off and got himself killed on the eve of the Armistice. As if it was his own fault and he could not wait. Joe had come from this town, a mystery to them then, and he was a good lad, they always said, but he had funny ideas. These were Socialist ones and they were contained in the writings which Ernie eagerly sct to reading. They were essays written for an evening class tutor. Ernie also read the book which was William Morris' *News from Nowhere*. Inside its cover there was an inscription written in a large casual hand: *Robert Jervis gave this book to Joe Buller*. His father's name came to him as a stranger's. Yet it was his own.

When he asked his grandma about the essays she shook her head,

'He was such a nice clean lad only ever so shy. Your mam was crackers about him, silly article, but it was easy to see why. Pity you dunna take after him—in looks, I mean. Not that you take after her either—you're more like your grandad's side. I think your grandad would've put them things in the ash-bidden if it hadna been for promising your mam and and Mr. Jervis's name being inside that book. He was the old Earl's nephew —such a clever lad, he's a professor now at Oxford. That's where your dad said he'd go one day—when the workers had justice done them he said. He was always saying things like that—worried your grandad to death. He said the war was the rich man's war and not the workers' and instead of killing German soldiers, he said, we should really be shaking hands with them—you should've seen your grandad's face when he said that —well he could've got had up for it. But nobody ever trampled on *him*. I wished your grandad had been a bit more like that instead of quiet—like you.'

Reading the essays was a disappointment to Ernie: he had expected too much from the copper-plate writing. It was *News from Nowhere* that brought him close to the dead man: the underlinings and margin-notes were like the tones of a voice speaking close at hand. The lad saw in a flash how the ideal world that William Morris

52

described had moved the young soldier of 1918. He was moved himself, seeing what it stood in accusation of: his own miserable job amid the miseries of the jobless. For he had had to leave school and give up the idea of studying at a music college. He found work with an assurance agency and went collecting door to door. The 'cash' he took in was payment off 'cheques' that his firm lent their customers for 'clothing and supply' from certain grim shops. In fine weather he rode an old bike which incorporated bits of his father's. His grandad had built it up for him from scrap, and Ernie felt it joined him with the dead men. When it rained he wore his near-ankle-length funerary gaberdine and carried a large black umbrella, one segment of which hung limp, skewered by a spoke. Sheila had laughed with loathing when she saw him like this. He knew it, and went out of his way to avoid her.

With the numbers on the dole, it became hopeless trying to get weekly payments. The customers pleaded poverty and sometimes shouted filth at him as if he were the cause of it all. He remembered how somebody once said Liddy's mother had killed herself to get out of debt. It seemed very likely. He made no commission because he got no new clients. He lost lots of old ones, in fact, and became an object of contempt to both sides. Yet he was terrified of losing the job, so that fear seemed to him the main feature of a working life.

If only his dad were alive, then they could stand together. He felt so alone in his growing thoughts.

He enrolled in the W.E.A. evening class in Politics and became one of its most faithful members. Then he joined the Labour Party, carefully explaining to his grandma how Socialism was the practical worldly form

53

of Christianity and you couldn't have one without the other.

'*I* can,' she said sharply, having heard him out.

When he went on the W.E.A. School at Oxford, Ernie felt, for the first time in his life, that he was at the hub of things instead of trudging round the edge. Leather-elbowed men jabbed their pipes into the air, their every word a thrust to action, while short-haired no-nonsense women in ankle socks took copious notes and asked pertinent questions that got issues defined to the bone. The towers and cloisters of the town seemed to have lain in wait for him all his life. He took his seat in a hall where all the great men who had eaten there looked out of the wainscot at him; he went to a bed which during term-time was slept in by a certain Honourable Somebody-Something; best of all, he was permitted to play the College Chapel organ to his heart's content.

But why shouldn't you? The voice that spoke inside him sounded more like Sheila's than his own. And it echoed what many of the student-workers on the course said as they drained their tankards and enjoyed being waited on by the impassive college servants. Why the hell shouldn't I, Ernie muttered to himself dutifully, unconvinced. Deference had been bred too far back in him. When he sat at the organ and saw through its mirror the Chapel vault arching in and out of time behind him, he believed he was, momentarily, in William Morris' Nowhere.

He had brought the book with him and set it up with others on the Honourable's shelves, alongside a heap of old invitation cards to sherry and Hunt Balls. He slipped one of the cards into his book to show his grandma. He could not understand why, like her, he was so glad to know that the aristocrats went grandly on with the pattern of their lives. There was something beautiful to him about the ghosts—ghosts processing back in time, like mirrors reflecting each other—who had lived their high lives in these rooms. Lives so unlike his own, ways he would never know. He did not want to know them, for he guessed that if he did, he would see their likeness to his own and be disappointed in them. He wanted so much to believe that there could be a better life.

It was the same with the dons. He imagined them poring over the chained books in Duke Humphrey's Library. He loved to see lights on behind lattice windows in turrets. Particularly he liked to think of the donor of *News from Nowhere* quietly at work in some dim, beamed room. With very deliberate casualness he asked one of his tutors which college Robert Jervis was a Fellow of. The answer came so easily, so off-handedly that Ernie took it almost as an omen, beckoning him to make himself known to the don.

So one evening he walked through the warm moonlight straight into Robert Jervis' college, asked the porter where he might find him and was directed to the garden quad. He stopped at the entry to the stairway and wondered what he was doing. He hadn't even brought the book to prove who he was. He began to make his way back to the gatehouse, but stopped again under the Chapel wall, looking up at the moon over the pinnacles. He thought of Sheila and how she would laugh at him for dithering. Thinking of her, too, made him feel suddenly homesick. Oxford and the course were nothing to his feelings for home. He longed to slip back into what he had come from, as a beetle might into the cracks of the stone under his hand.

At last he tiptoed up the staircase to the top landing and stood at the door. There was a line of light under it and music coming from behind it. A pleasant baritone voice was singing in German:

Du bist die Ruh', du bist der Frieden,
du bist vom Himmel mir beschieden—

'Oh hell! Why do I always do that?'

The pianist faltered and the song was stopped. Muttering came now from behind the door, then the piano phrase, then the phrase again with the voice, then silence again. A slither of steps came and the door opened on Ernie cringing against the bannisters. A small fine face peered out with minimal interest.

'Oh, I thought it was my scout. You haven't seen him, I suppose?'

'No—I——'

They looked at each other for a few nonplussed seconds. Ernie was the one who made the effort, tremendous for him:

'Was that Schumann?'

The don nodded, agreeably surprised.

'I can't ever get that damned bit right. Did you hear?'

'Yes.'

'I'm Robert Jervis. Who're you?'

'Ernie—I mean, Ernest Hordell, I mean Ernest Buller. I came to see you.'

'Come in then. Why are you standing out here? Did somebody send you?'

'No—not really. I've got a book of yours, but—I've forgotten to bring it with me.'

'Oh *well*.' Jervis raised his hand and shrugged. Then he looked hard at Ernie who shifted and twisted his neck.

'D'you play by any chance?' Jervis had noticed the youth's spidery fingers and nodded at the grand piano that, black and shiny, had a vase of deep red gladioli on it and a green-shaded lamp. It was a room full of soft pools of light and softer shadows.

'Yes, a bit. About this book——'

'Forget it. Look, you couldn't just sketch the piano bit in for me, could you? I can't seem to sing and do that as well.'

'I'll have a go.'

Ernie went to the piano and sat down, hardly crediting that he was where he was.

They went through the song three times. Jervis held his notes firmly and seemed ready to applaud himself.

'You're good—really, very good.'

Ernie flushed and felt happy and warm.

'Scotch?' Jervis asked when they sat back in the velvet arm-chairs.

Ernie shook his head, puzzled at the irrelevance of the question.

Jervis nodded, his eyes crinkling slightly. He tried again, more explicitly and as if moving on to a new idea.

'I expect you'd like a drink, wouldn't you?'

Ernie's blood rushed to his face as he realised what the previous question had meant, and he straightaway became his old unconfident self again.

'What would you like?'

'Scotch,' said the boy hoarsely, as if snatching a word from the air.

Jervis went and pushed open a little window and smiled broadly into the plane-tree lit by his room's lamps. Then he moved to a cupboard. Ernie sat back weakly and gazed round the room. It was the best he had ever been in. There was the portrait of a man in sober seventeenth-century clothes over the fireplace and mellow landscapes on the other walls. Eastern carpets set off the furniture, and antique sculptures lay casually around. Ernie looked particularly at a seated draped figure, headless, one broken hand stroking the worn body of an animal.

'That's mother,' Jervis smiled. Ernie looked very doubtful, so, 'Cybele,' he explained further.

'Oh.' Ernie tried to look knowing. It couldn't even have been a *weathered* statue of Mr. Jervis' mother, he was sure of that.

'She was from Selham, wasn't she? I mean, your mother.'

He laughed awkwardly.

'Yes.' Jervis looked pleasantly surprised as he handed Ernie his whisky. 'How d'you know?'

'I come from near there.'

'Not the Potteries?'

'Yes.' Ernie laughed again, feeling it was something to apologise for.

'I ought to have guessed. The accent. Now it comes back to me.'

'Have I got it then?' Ernie thought he had mastered a quite neutral speech.

'Unmistakably. Don't go and tell me you're ashamed of it. It's a damn good thing.' Jervis said this to all his working-class students and they believed him. 'Are you on a Miners' scholarship by any chance?'

'Oh, if only I was. Just the W.E.A. Summer School that's all.'

'Then how did you get hold of my book? Are you sure it's mine?' Jervis looked oddly at him. 'What is it, by the way?'

'*News from Nowhere.*'

'*News from Nowhere*? I don't remember—just a minute—just a minute——'

'Selham. It was 1917.'

'One of the servants.'

'No. My father. He was just visiting. He wasn't a servant.'

'Of course not. There was a girl——'

'My mother.'

'The young man was a bit older than me. He went to the war, didn't he?'

'Got killed in France, yes.'

'Oh.'

'I never knew my father.'

'So your mother sent you?'

Ernie shook his head smiling apologetically.

'No, she died as well. It was my grandad who kept the book. He was one of the keepers at Selham. It's a pleasure-park now.'

'I know. I've never been back since the family sold up.' He pointed at the portrait over the hearth. 'I salvaged my goodness knows how many times great grandfather from auction. Selham wouldn't have got sold, though, if it hadn't been for the War.'

'So there's no heir now.'

'Oh yes, my cousin Ted—but there's nothing much for him to inherit. As a matter of fact he's up at the moment—he's about your age.'

The clear voice on the whisky and rose scented air spoke as if Selham were the whole world and Ernie had no difficulty in accepting the view. Embedded in cushions, he did not notice the time until it was too late. When he did he broke into near-panic.

'They lock up at eleven. I shan't be able to get in. What shall I do?'

Jervis looked at him in surprise and with a twinge of distaste.

'You could climb in,' he sighed drily. 'Everybody does.'

'Oh no, I couldn't do that.'

'Well, I suppose it's a bit tricky, if you don't have the technique. Wait a minute, will you?'

The don slipped from the room. Ernie stood helpless and heedless of everything but his plight, his eyes fixed on the clock until Mr. Jervis came back, saying,

'I've phoned a friend in your college. He'll let you in. Come on. I'll see you—safely—through the garden-gate.'

Ernie's pleasure in the evening came back to him. On the lawn of the Fellows' Garden a group of small white iron chairs and tables glowed like skeletons of Edwardian undergraduates. It was as if the flowers had put all their being into the air, it was so heavy. Ernie lagged behind to hold what he thought would be his last sight of the scene, and Jervis stopped, surprised again at the youth's emotions, which in turn moved him.

'You must come to tea one day before you go back to the Potteries. What about Friday? If it keeps fine, we'll have it out here.'

'That'd be marvellous—but are you sure? I mean—I don't want to be a nuisance.'

'I don't ask nuisances twice.' Jervis was not so certain as his tone.

They shook hands. Ernie walked quickly, still in a

dream, through the hushed streets. Crossing Radcliffe Square, he touched a crevice of its Camera, this Oxford being as much a part of him now as of any of its own.

Before he went to tea with Robert Jervis, Ernie had to rehearse a song with a Manchester girl called Brenda Whitehead. It was for the concert which the course-members regularly got up as their parting occasion. Brenda was disconcertingly squat, and Ernie did not like the way she gave looks down at his fly-hole and then up into his face, or her frizzy hair under his nose. It was unpleasant to sit at the piano and have her parrotty face level with his own while she stood and warbled *When I Grow too Old to Dream*. She insisted on frequent rehearsals and wherever he went, she was liable to be lurking just round the corner. She kept him a place at every meal and made a bee-line for him whenever he appeared in the Common Room. Yet he never deliberately avoided her, because he sensed that she stood to him as he did to Sheila. But he writhed with resentment and embarrassment when she came and studied the music with him, her hair occasionally pricking against his chin and a monthly kind of smell whisking from her movements. To make up for her size, her voice was tremendous and when it rang out, drowning the piano, Ernie heard windows being banged shut round the quad.

'Yes, I'd've been on the stage if I'd've only been a bit bigger,' Brenda said, having finished her singing.

'I think you would too.'

His heart went out to her until she suddenly screwed her head round and said,

'Now what shall we do?'

'I've got to go to tea.' His relief was almost blatant. 'One of the dons asked me.'

'Oh, I say, we *are* moving in high circles, aren't we? Well, you'll be sure to be back in good time for the concert, won't you?'

'Of course I shall.'

'I suppose I'll take a walk round Magdalen then—just me and meself and I—seeing there's nobody else wants to go with me.'

Her nose seemed to curve further into her lip and she looked even smaller and sharper. Ernie's heart clinched with his alien feelings. Why did his response as a man have to be so different from his response as a human being? She stood with her arms folded and watched him slip deferentially through the door. He did not see her make a face at its shutting, or hear the irritable sigh through her nose as she shrugged,

'He's not that much cop, anyway.'

The youth was thankful to get out into the bright air. In that room he had been wrenched back to dismalness. Now he saw all too clearly why Sheila had been hard and scornful with him. Something about sex made one like that. He had been hard, too, and yet cowardly at the same time. He felt hot and prickly.

Robert Jervis was waiting for him in the garden. A scout brought the silver tea-things out to them. The cedar under which they sat looked like eastern writing on the sky. Ernie's eyes watered at the dazzling starkness of the scene and were held by the two figures dodging and giggling away down the lawn. A portable gramophone lay open on the grass, with scattered records, one broken.

'My cousin and his fiancée will join us, I expect, when they get bored with croquet.'

A white-shirted, white-trousered blond young man stood aiming with his mallet, and a dark girl in a white frock with black spots and high puff sleeves lifted her tanned arms. Sometimes they twined round the white-shirted body, which shook them off. Then they stretched in the air and the girl twirled in and out of the trees. Ernie dizzied in heat and pleasure. He felt hollow too, with a sense of not really being part of it, of being a grey intrusion where everything else fitted so perfectly.

'And what have you been doing with yourself since I last saw you?'

'We've been rehearsing for our social.'

'Your *social?*'

Perhaps, thought Ernie, I am a nuisance to him, after all. He wished they were indoors so that he could justify himself again at the piano. He saw that he had nothing else to offer. Four brown arms wreathed in the sunshine and four eyes were fixed in focus on them.

The youth shouted,

'That's it. I've won.'

'You cheated,' the girl cried with a slight Scottish accent. 'I wasn't looking.'

She went for him playfully, and he drew her to him in a laughing kiss. Robert Jervis and Ernie exchanged forced child-tolerating smiles.

'Stop it, you two. Come and have some tea.'

Moist and flushed, the pair dashed up, alive as flowers of the border. Ernie felt paralysed by the attack of their good looks and was actually paralysed by having his sandwich plate and teacup perched on his knees. He shrank, not being able to get up for the lady as Jervis so easily did. He half raised a timid hand and then lowered it at the absence of a corresponding interest.

'It's no use playing any sort of game with an immoralist like Ted. He doesn't recognise rules. You should hit him with the mallet when he cheats. You let him get away with things.'

'Don't we all?'

Everybody laughed, including Ernest—as if he were one of them.

Ted kissed the girl briefly and then knelt to put a record on the gramophone. It was *I'll See You Again*.

They all listened dreamily. Ernie felt the hair on his neck tingle. Then,

'We had it in the punt—it was lovely,' said the girl.

'I'm sure it was,' Jervis said.

They all laughed and the girl's smile flashed indiscriminately across Ernie's face. He smiled back long after it was necessary and sweated like mad. Her dark hair and straight look reminded him of Sheila. But there was all the difference in the world in the air this girl brought with her. There was no crudity, no harshness: the air was not smoky and Woolworth's-scented but light and fragrant. Elizabeth's dress blossomed round her and there were none of those acrid wafts that spiked from Brenda. At least he didn't think so. It was easy to see why she did not notice him at all. The blond youth was unlike anyone else of his own age that Ernie had ever met. It wasn't just a matter of fine features, brown eyes and brown skin making his blondness the more striking; every gesture he made and every expression that crossed his face seemed drawn in a design, a destiny. Here were people not doomed to frustration or waiting on accident but moving naturally to fulfilment, like figures in an opera. Ernie was not envious or politically roused; he was, simply, amazed and delighted that ideals could come true.

They chattered on about their game, how they intended to spend the long vac. and what a bore it was that their Salzburg trip was off because of the *Anschluss*. During the talk Ernie found himself eating all the sandwiches in a kind of nervous frenzy. There were the last two on his plate, both bitten into. He blushed and sweated but nobody *seemed* to notice. He had his cup automatically replenished by Jervis and sat back trying to appear intelligently interested. Jervis suddenly coughed.

'What is it you're doing on your course, Mr. Hordell?'

Ted put his tongue into the mouth of a cream-horn and said, 'Mmm.'

'Well, it goes under the general title of *Capital and Labour 1880 to 1935.*'

'Goodness!' Everyone looked at Elizabeth when she said this, and she stretched her neck as if preparing to listen most intently. 'It must be terribly interesting.' The girl fingered the hair on her neck.

'Yes,' Ernie nodded vigorously and smiled across at Ted who sighed into his tea-cup and said,

'We're driving up to town this evening, Robert. Coming?'

'Oh—I hadn't reckoned—I really should do some work on Callimachus.'

'Oh, Robert, you're so funny. Callimachus—*honestly*!'

'We'll be meeting Fiona. Did you know that Ian was back?'

'No—when?'

The talk took another turn which Ernie could not follow. The splendid trio became engrossed in a life of its own that seemed the only thing of importance to it.

It was one thing and he was another. He sat ignored, but nonetheless admiring, seeing life at last as he thought it was meant to be. Eventually Jervis turned with his reassuring smile.

'I'm so sorry, Mr. Hordell. It was rude of us to go on like that. Didn't you say you had a concert-party this evening? So you probably won't mind if I let myself be whisked off to town by these little devils.'

Ernie nodded and gave a smile that seemed to apologise for his still being there.

'The only thing is,' Jervis went on, 'when shall we have another meeting?'

Ernie shook his head.

'I'm off tomorrow. It'll have to be next year. I don't suppose you ever come up to Stoke these days.'

'Oh dear no,' Jervis laughed.

Ernie laughed, too, at the notion.

'Next year, then.'

He wanted to turn and take in the scene, which he guessed would not repeat itself in his experience, but he dared not for fear of seeming inquisitive. Only when he got into the darkness of the passage to the cloister did he look back. Elizabeth was placing a white blazer over Ted's shoulders, having wrapped her head in a gauzy blue scarf. Then both took Robert by the arm, smiling persuasively at him. They moved across the lawn and along the colonnade of the lovely building, appearing and disappearing, seeming inseparable.

No matter how much he might disapprove of Ted's manners, that was how, Ernie said to himself, he would have liked to be. That was how a life should be. He felt such aching for impossibilities and, at the same time, again a twinge of homesickness. He needed to go back into the home of his ugliness. But before that could be, he had the ordeal of the Social to go through. He had to face Brenda again.

The show seemed to Ernie a parade of freaks and he knew he was one of them. It began with a Russian folksong given by a couple of Communists who had lately been on a Co-op trip to Moscow and never stopped talking about it. Their song was about a tank. Its audience seemed glad of a chance to display collective bleakness. The singers were very crestfallen at the response and Ernie felt sorry for them. A corny Lancashire monologue came next. Unamused, people muttered and even interjected so that the reciter fumbled over his few jokes. Brenda, coming to take her possessive stand by Ernie's side, grimaced,

'Did you ever?'

Ernie turned his eyes from her and thought of Elizabeth's smooth arms and twirling body, of *I'll See You Again,* and of the trio driving up to London in an open car, laughing together about him.

A sweaty-moustached girl quavered sweetly through *Where e'er you walk* and somehow moved everybody, more than moved Ernie, such music spinning him to a sphere beyond even that of Ted and Elizabeth.

A strange pair took the stage to give a scene from Shakespeare. They were said to be having a sneaky affair. If so, this was their only consummation. The bald and runty Antony played to his acid electric Cleopatra with such intensity as to put everybody in a state of sweaty turmoil. Especially Ernie, who grew ever more conscious of the gap between ideal forms and their crippled shadows.

When his and Brenda's turn came, he saw his painful

awkward self bending above the gleaming dwarf who gripped his hand and swung him into the piano seat. They began with *Oh Wandering One*. Brenda rocketed through its coloratura, astonishing the house.

The applause was terrific and she seemed to swell, though not upwards. *When I Grow too Old to Dream* was an equal success, with Brenda laying her hands pumpingly on Ernie's shoulders and putting her head on one side in budgerigar fashion. There was nothing for it, there had to be an encore. Ernie found the sheet of *I'll See You Again* being nudged into his hand by Brenda, who was grinning with hideous excitement and whispering,

'You know this, don't you?'

Ernie's fingers froze to a pianissimo as if to excuse himself from sacrilege. The audience swung heftily into the melody, conducted by Brenda who was now swaying in ecstasy. It was repeated *ad nauseam*. Gigantic clapping hammered Ernie's head, which Brenda suddenly snatched between her hands, dragging it to her brooch-sharp blouse. She gave it a smacking kiss. People roared approval. Ernie almost fainted. He rose red and shuddering and scuttled from the platform, down the aisle, out through the door and far into the quiet town, anywhere away from laughter and clapping and the gripping girl. What hurled him forward was his sense of them all acknowledging that he belonged with her. Just as Ted belonged with Elizabeth. The beautiful to the beautiful. The ugly to the ugly. Ted, Elizabeth, Oxford. The Potteries, Brenda, himself.

He ran down towards Christ Church. But that was Ted's college, as its swanky gateway seemed to proclaim. So he turned off into the back streets, glad to find dim terraces that reminded him of home. He felt himself acknowledged by these streets and his self-possession began to come back. He went into a pub and was reassured by the disregard of the boozers. After a pint he felt better and, reflecting that it was his first pint in a pub on his own, he had another and felt better still. Did he *always* have to be the victim of the way things were? Could he not be the master of them sometimes? That was what Teddy clearly was: master of things. To go about and do what one wanted and not care, that was the way to be, that was living. He could have learned it from Sheila. Doing what one didn't want, being anxious all the while, that was death. If he could only be like Teddy. Like Sheila. He slapped his mug and money down for another pint, but when it was full he felt he didn't want it after all. He had to sip it very steadily, every drop, as he had been brought up to waste not. He longed to chat casually with the men around him, but he could not. Everything got together to make him less than a man. As images blurred in his mind, Teddy mingled with Sheila mocking his lack. What was it that could make one person so totally different from another? Teddy would cast a spell over everybody, even here, draw all eyes to him, and his Elizabeth would wind herself round him. While Ernie cringed in the corner of his small self. And now Brenda came back into his mind. He had let her down in front of everybody. His heart sank, spongy with pity.

At closing time he blundered out into the night, his yeasty breath about him. He came against a massive dark wall by the river, crumbling, dandelion-festooned and disregarded. At its raggy top there was a broken tower with a star shining through its window. He shivered as

69

the memory of visiting such a ruin as a child with Sheila came back to him. The stones were so formless, though, that it seemed far older than any of the college buildings he had seen, as if it had been there since the beginning of settlements. Why its knobbly cavities should give him a feeling of strength beyond himself he never rightly knew. He wandered back into the town-lights. It was his last time in Oxford, yet he felt he was not so much saying good-bye to it as taking it into himself. But panic soon crumpled the strength when he realised he had gone beyond gate-closing time again. He rushed towards the college like a mad horse, then stopped himself short.

'What if I have? It's warm enough to stay out all night.'

Somehow, though, now that he said it, he didn't seem to want to stay out all night. The idea of bed grew more and more alluring. He wandered along under the college walls and came to where a lamp-post stood up against the crenellations. A spiky frill jutted at the point of contact. It would be easy for somebody like Teddy to just climb in. Why not for me then? He hugged himself round the lamp-post and started to shin up but dropped back, loose with beery weariness. He tried again and managed to reach the spikes, which he clung to, frantic with the effort and ready to give up at any second. Footsteps up the street made him momentarily superhuman with terror and he twisted himself painfully round the frill. One spike tore at his trouser-leg.

'My best suit,' he moaned, though the spike had also gashed his calf.

Now he was on the wall's crest, a long drop the other side. From the street a voice burred up,

'Can I help you, sir?'

70

A constable's torch-beam flashed into his pale face. Scent of stocks rushed at him and his knee buckled to give his chin a tongue-splitting crack. He lay shaking for a while, tears watering the crushed flowers.

'I've broken me back. I've broken me back. Whatever will me grandma say? Me best suit's all ripped. Oh, God, whatever shall I do?'

But he had not broken his back, and he was surprised, even disappointed, to find that he did not faint when he creaked to his feet. He lurched off to his room and there cried himself to sleep.

He woke very early at the singing of the birds, a keen throb in his leg and tongue. He cleaned himself up and got his pyjamas on and tried to get back to sleep. But he could not catch it now, so he sat in the window-seat of the room he had grown so fond of during the week and watched the sun rise over the chapel tower and blackbirds skim across the lawns and back. In spite of his pain, he felt triumphant now. There would surely be a to-do when the porter found out. The police would come and identify him. All the same he had done it: he had climbed in, like any hothead undergrad. It would be worth the exposure for people to know he had a will of his own. From now on things were going to be very different.

When at last he made a terrific effort to enter the hall for breakfast, nobody particularly noticed him. He blinked round, scared of meeting Brenda's eyes. There they were, skinned for him, unavoidable. He slid on to her bench and waited for it.

'Wherever did you get to last night? We looked everywhere. You silly coot, running off like that in front of everybody. It wasn't very nice, you know.'

'I just wanted some fresh air.'

'You do pay the most charming compliments, I must say.'

'I'm sorry, Brenda. It wasn't you—honest.'

She merely sliced the crusts off her toast.

So she didn't know anything—yet.

'You weren't even there at midnight—I know that for a fact. The club met—it was a party and ever so nice—wasn't it, Mu?'

She turned to her neighbour who nodded indifferently.

'I came and knocked at your door, but you weren't there—were you?'

He admitted it. Brenda carefully snicked peel out of her marmalade.

'Where were you then?'

'I just walked around.'

Brenda took a wash of tea to the last gnashings of her toast and swallowed. Her eyes waited until the mouthful had sunk well into her gullet, then they turned on him with a new expression.

'Really, Ernie, if you don't mind my saying so, you'll go funny always doing things on your own.'

Ernie allowed his tea to steam his glasses up.

'How d'*you* know I do them on me own?'

The look that cut across her face made him wish his words unsaid. They sat in silence a while, their eating and drinking actions seeming to be over-deliberate.

'What time's your train?' he asked at last.

'You know very well—it's the same as yours till Wolverhampton. We both change there, you know. Hoping to get rid of me, were you?'

His heart sank.

'We don't have to say good-bye yet then.'

'Well, we could go at different times, I daresay. Wait till later. I'm sure I don't mind. You might have got somebody else to go with for all I know.'

He tried to laugh.

'I'll see you at the lodge then—at quarter to.'

'Okey-doke.'

He got up and she cocked her eyes at his legs as usual.

'What *have* you done to your trousers? They're all ripped.'

Everybody looked. He didn't know what to say at first. Then, as he realised that nobody would ever know about his escapade if he didn't tell them himself, he said,

'Oh, I had to climb in last night. I tore 'em on the lamp-post.'

'You what?'

'I climbed in the college.' He beamed.

'I'd better mend them for you. You can't go home in that state. Your best suit and all.'

'Never mind—doesn't matter.'

'Yes, it does. Come on. I've got a thread in my room.'

He deflated at this, following her meekly and worrying in case he didn't have time to go to the lavatory properly.

She seemed unnecessarily delighted at having to sew his trousers, and there was a bit of banter as to whether he should take them off or not. He couldn't decide which would be less embarrassing: to stand in Brenda's room without them or to have her fingers twiddling round his legs. He took them off at last and whipped her bath towel round him to hide, as he told himself, his gash. Brenda doubled up laughing and pointing at him. The old scout chose that moment to come in. He politely

73

turned round and went out again as if he had forgotten something. Another knock at the door preceded Muriel's head poking round it, saying,

'Just looked in to say—coo, you've got him where you want him, I see.'

Ernie shuffled and his red miserable smile took on deeper shades of redness and misery.

'He ripped his trousers climbing in last night,' Brenda tittered with happy pride, biting her cotton. 'And Muggins has got to do him up.'

Ernie tried to look as if he had won a medal at Berlin or something, as Muriel's quick eyes summed him up, only to drop him flat.

' A likely story! Well, I must rush. There's five of us sharing a taxi and it'll be waiting and clocking up. Toodle-oo. See you next year.'

She blew them a kiss of dismissal and was gone.

'There, they're done.'

Brenda playfully threw the trousers at him. In jerking to catch them, he lost his towel.

'Just look at your leg.'

Hesitantly, as if it were not his own, he looked. He saw the red-slashed white lath that extended from his baggy underpants.

'What did you have to go and do that for? It's a good job I've got a plaster with me. Eeh, you are a one, aren't you?'

'It doesn't matter. It's O.K. now. Fresh air's best for it.'

'Fresh air? Doesn't look as though your legs have seen fresh air in donkey's years.'

She damped some cotton wool, then knelt to rummage in her case and brought out the plaster. She ran on her knees to him and looked up with a mocking smile. He backed but she caught him round the ankle.

'Come on. Don't be daft.'

They struggled for a few moments. Twisting on one leg, he had a sudden impulse to kick out at her face. But he did not do it. She dabbed her cotton wool on him and then slammed the plaster on, raising a cry from him.

'Ooh, men *are* soft things.'

She laughed very oddly and grasped him round his knees. Then she gave her bird-look up at him. He panicked. She laughed very loudly.

'You thought I was going to kiss your knobbly knees, didn't you?'

He didn't know what he had thought. She howled with laughter. It seemed almost worse than kisses.

'You vain thing—you really thought I wanted to kiss your horrible knees. Ugh—*men!*'

Her violent shuddering movement made him fall against the toilet-table. The water from its bowl slopped over on to the girl and stopped her guffawing.

He hurried into his trousers, found they were back to front and got them off again just in time for the re-entry of the scout who had been patiently waiting and listening just outside the door. He mopped up as if such scenes were routine. When he had gone out, Brenda began to cry.

'I don't know what makes me like that. Doctor says it's me glands, but I don't know. If only——'

'What?' he asked kindly, his hands twitching to comfort her. 'What is it?'

She did not speak, only looked far into the sky, and he dared not risk misinterpretation so he only stood there.

'I suppose I'd better go and pack. Shall I see you at the lodge? I'll carry your case to the station.'

She nodded, wiping her eyes with her towel.

On the journey to Wolverhampton they hardly spoke, but from time to time each glanced seekingly at the other and then away when the other looked back. If only there wasn't sex, Ernie thought, as he looked at her blackish fuzz and cramped body, and then at his bony hands on his meatless thighs. If only.

When they parted Brenda snuffled a bit again.

'It's like this always. You know, I live for that week at Oxford—all the year through—then when it comes, it's hell—because you don't—there's just nothing—Shall you write to me?'

He nodded solemnly and handed her her case.

IX

Marriage is not for me, Sheila said. None of the lads she knew was fit for spending a lifetime with. It seemed best not to get to know a fellow too well as he generally turned out to be a big let-down. A Robert Taylor type across the dance-floor could make her quiver like a bird, but once they got in close-up she would go right off him.

Her latest boy was the safe type. He was the Post-mistress' son, a mother's boy so everybody said. How she had got in with him was a mystery still to Sheila. Of course it was on the rebound, her usual state. Roger, waiting for the bounce, followed her wherever she went, and pestered and meithered. His car was at her disposal, there were chocolates and silk stockings galore, trips here, there and everywhere.

It took some time before she had to pay for these things by letting herself be kissed. Even then he put it so politely.

'Would you mind—I mean—if—can I just—you know——?' and she smiled a regal yes, thinking there was more to come than there was and surprised at her disappointment. Robert wasn't bad-looking, though baby-faced inevitably and rather too well-groomed. It irritated her how readily men fell into their types.

But Roger wasn't as predictable as she thought.

'I could kill my mother,' he muttered one night as they were driving home in the dark.

'Oh, you shouldn't say a thing like that,' Sheila said, agreeably startled.

'I could, honest. She's spoiled my life.'

'Get away with you—she's given you everything you want.'

'Not everything. Not the main thing. I'm not a man, you know, not properly.'

He sniffed as if tearful and stopped the car. Oh heck, Sheila thought, we're going to have confessions. When men got intimate and dramatic she wanted to giggle. They would speak in low voices far away from the subject that was really on their minds. She could see every step in advance and would soon get bored by the process. They would pick at her cardigan and pat her cheek as if they only wanted to be her favourite brother. But Roger amazed her by being sudden and direct.

'Will *you* make me a man, Sheila? I mean now?'

'Oh, I think we'd better get back home, Rodge. Me mother'll be waiting up.'

'It won't take long.'

How do *you* know, she wanted to ask. How typical of a man to think only of his own time.

'P'raps another day.'

'No, now.'

He was getting breathy and pushing. She wasn't sure whether she liked it or not, though it was certainly unexpected.

'Ooh, ey up,' she said when he launched his full body on hers. She opened the door of the car and they both fell out in a puddle. 'It's all mucky down here.'

She picked herself up and ran round a tree, trying to decide what she wanted to do. She hadn't reckoned on this eventuality just now. As she touched the branches of the tree and felt leaves brush by her, sex seemed a foolish thing, more childish than childhood. An owl hooted and she dashed back to the car. If it was the only way to get home, she might as well give in.

Gazing at the orange moon while he worked himself up on her, she strangely wished that, like it, she didn't have to be bothered with life. The romance was never what it promised to be.

But this time it almost was. For Roger was an expert at love. She knew straightaway it was by no means his first time. The bloody hypocrite, she thought, gladly snuggling to his warm pudgy baby's sort of body.

Sheila's partner on Woolworth's cosmetic counter was Maureen, a fat freckled girl of sixteen. She would gaze at Roger as if he were the world's wonder. Not that he ever noticed her. Nor did the other fellows who came to flirt with Sheila, which both flattered and annoyed the older girl. It was a satisfied, patronising sort of annoyance she could afford to feel. It seemed wrong that nobody should notice Maureen or take her anywhere when she was obviously dying to be asked. So one day Sheila insisted on Roger's asking her out with them on one of their drives in the country.

'After all,' she said, when he showed unwilling, 'she doesn't have to be in the car with us.'

'No, there's no room. So that settles it.'

'But you've got that funny little seat in the boot.'

'The dickie?'

'Yes, we'll squeeze her in there.'

'Suppose we can't get her out once she's in?'

'P'raps she'll come in useful as a spare tyre—or two.'

Roger's loud guffaw made Sheila realise yet again how

silly and biddable men were. But he wasn't that easily persuaded. Lightly he said,

'She can come if.'

'If what?'

'This.'

He produced a small box which he flicked open to reveal a ring with a cluster of specky diamonds.

'Ooh.'

The ring seemed to flash with all his capacity to make her life luxurious. She let him put it on her finger, though she actually said and thought nothing. She could not bear to look at his gleeful face but scrutinised the ring instead, thinking she would go and get it valued the next day. She wasn't sure she would keep it, but it would be nice to wear it for a while.

When she saw Maureen's gasping pleasure at the prospect of the drive she wished she hadn't made such a joke of it. Nor was it finally all that much of a joke stuffing her into the boot. Yet she was hysterically happy even at the discomfort, and Sheila could have cried.

'It's a good job she's well-sprung,' Roger grinned. 'She'll be that jogged I only hope we don't find her melted down when we get there.'

Sheila did not laugh with him this time, but he was so pleased with himself he didn't notice. She felt very guilty when, at the journey's end, Maureen climbed out less healthy-looking than she had gone in.

They picnicked on the moors towards Buxton, but Maureen was a bit off her food and shy with Roger. She seemed scared too by the empty spike-green spaces all around, cut by dark red rocks splitting at the sheer sky. Grouse squawked up about her as she trod fearfully into this foreign world, and a fox streaked sudden and ginger, across her sight. Roger stole a kiss or two but could not get down to what he called 'serious necking' with Sheila because Maureen scurried back to them at every tiny fright. Sheila thoroughly enjoyed his frustration. It was just what she wanted, to spoil his all-too-predictable plans. His rights, no doubt he thought, now she was chained by his diamond ring. Well, he had another think coming. This wasn't her idea of love at all, and she was getting very fed up with the dent of his penis against her flanks.

'Hell's bells,' he snarled, seeing Maureen emerge on to the horizon for the umpteenth time, growing fatter at each gallop. 'I'll wring her bloody neck before the day's out.'

'Don't be selfish. After all, we can do this sort of thing any time.'

'We'll do it tonight, just as soon as we've got rid of Fatso.'

That's what you think, she tightly smiled to herself, saying,

'So why're you mucking me about now?'

She straightened her clothes self-absorbedly. He looked at her and saw a totally hostile being whom he did not know at all. Sometimes he loathed the way she talked. It seemed deliberately to reduce things. He felt afraid, noticing for once the solitude of the gullies above them and the iron rims of the hills. He touched her thigh for assurance, but she stiffened, glancing up at Maureen with a bright smile,

'Are you enjoying yourself, duck?'

Maureen nodded an automatic nod like a moor-hen. Her life was made up of catching other people making love and she didn't enjoy it particularly. She yearned for her home as if she were billions of miles away from it.

'Did you find the little waterfall like I told you?' Roger asked sharply.

'No. I daren't go that far by meself after seeing that fox. You never know, there might be snakes and that.'

Roger laughed his silly laugh. He could have kicked himself for having scared her with snakes in the first place.

Sheila got up quickly and took Maureen's hand.

'Come on. I'll go with you. Coming, Roger?'

She wouldn't have asked him, only she knew he couldn't leave his precious car with the hood down and all their things strewn round. His mother had made him strictly security-conscious. He looked savagely at the girls, his teeth flashing in the sunlight.

'No. I'll pack up so we'll be ready for off when you get back. Don't be long, mind.'

We'll be as long as we damn well please were the words that rushed to Sheila's lips, but she swallowed them and gave him instead one of her brilliant smiles. And, as they walked away, she fastened her arm, with exaggerated fondness, round Maureen's shoulder, glancing back at the baffled baby-face of her lover. Maureen was also baffled and her shoulders tautened under the commanding hand.

But Sheila forgot about Roger and even about Maureen as they traced the narrow path between heather-tufts. Maureen kept flinching out of the way of bees, who had no interest in her whatsoever but were all for the purple bells. Sheila egged her forward relentlessly. The bracken grew thicker and more difficult to step over and thistles pricked their ankles. But Sheila broke through, pointing to a narrow dark rift in the earth ahead.

'There it is.'

She was excited, as if getting to the fall had been a terrific dare. She yanked Maureen over the hidden boulders. Bracken stalks tugged in raw twists round their legs, making Maureen cry out,

'It's a snake, I'm sure it's a snake.'

Sweat streaked her fiery face, but Sheila did not turn round to pull her on any more. She plunged forward like a fox pointed on prey.

They arrived scratched and blood-spotted, gasping, greasy.

'I was a fool to wear these stockings.'

Sheila scrutinised the shreds of tan silk, drawing her hand up to her thigh with a remote half-smiling shift of her eyes. How beautiful she is, Maureen thought. The gleam of sweat seemed just sunlight on her. I'm glad I can't see myself. I bet I look awful as usual.

What a sight Mo is, thought Sheila.

The waterfall was a small narrow thread of greeny whiteness set deep into the hill-cleft. Two boulders jutted at the crest of it and it fell like milky hair through a crimson bow. Both girls longed to drink at it forever, so fuddled they were by the sun. They gaped into the pebbly pool which caught the force, hypnotised by the glass stillness that lay outside its pounded core.

'Let's go up there.' Sheila pointed to the rocks at the fall's rim.

'Ooh, no, I anna gooing no further.'

Maureen fixed her eyes on the water and rooted herself where she was, her own will having drawn strength from what she saw. Sheila glanced at her in admiring surprise, irritated but glad that the other girl was not altogether to be led. Then she swung away, lightly climbing the steep rocks. She wove round a skirl of rowans, upwards, struck as never before by the glory of such trees that held their fists on the rock and went wild with so much colour and fruit. She came breathless to the point where the fall began and stood astride the jutting rocks, hailing the world. Maureen waved back, glad to have her friend in view again. Sheila gazed giddily down the spout of the force and thought of herself going with the long water, hammered into the pebbles of the pool before Maureen's pebbly eyes. She laughed to think of the girl having to go back and tell Roger. How helpless and wondering they would both be.

She screwed the engagement ring from her finger and held it above the water. What a laugh to say she had lost it in the falls. But it flashed in the sun and she felt its loveliness almost stabbing her. If only she could have bought it herself and it had not come from him. She slipped it into her pocket and shifted round to take in the view up and beyond. There were the hills called the Roches that she had seen long ago, seeming close enough to touch. She had known they were here and seen them often from further off, but somehow they seemed alive to her today. She remembered how once she had gone with Ernie and Judder, the barge-boy, and, running away from them, had seen these hills between foxgloves. The Roches. Shuttingsloe. The Roches. She had never been able to look at them since without an odd feeling. Something she could never fix her gaze on, never say what it was. It was in the blood-red rocks sheer against the sun and in that smooth green pike. It reached out at her.

84

'What the hell are you playing at?'

Roger's voice brayed across the heather, like a motor-horn. There was a short irrelevant screech from Maureen who had just gone behind a bush. Roger stood gesticulating. It was a good job he wasn't close enough to Sheila to see the look that changed her face. Maureen pulled her knickers up and scooted towards him.

'You'll have to come and help me down, darling,' Sheila cooed falsely.

She heard him swear and she turned away to smile twistily and to have the view to herself for a last minute or two. But she could not recover the live feeling: nothing was there now, save what did not regard her at all, and she was too conscious of her fiancé toiling and cursing his way up the slope.

'What did you damn well go and get yourself stuck up here for, you stupid cow?'

'I wanted to,' she began icily, but then, 'Just to see,' she added with a girlish flutter. So I'm a cow, am I?

He snatched her hand. She had one last glance at the hill-tops, then let him drag her down, pretending to be scared and clinging to him so that he was tugged against the rocks and grew livider at each step.

Maureen was already at the car, biting her nails.

'Oh, you've put the lid down.' Sheila knew he would have done. Otherwise wild horses wouldn't have dragged him from his machine.

'If you mean I've put the hood up, the answer's yes, and that's the way it's staying.'

'It's better open when it's hot.'

'It's staying closed.'

Sheila looked him up and down and, glazing her eyes, fixed them on his hips. He'll get fat, she decided, once he's married, he'll be the sort that's always having his trousers let out.

He wanted to cry. He wanted to hit her. She could hurt him as he had never been hurt by a girl before. Maureen stared from face to face. Sheila looked ready to go beserk but very sweetly,

'All right,' she said and with rigid calm began to climb into the boot.

'Not in there.' Roger's face bulged.

'But I want to go in there. It's only fair to Maureen. You said she'd get jiggered to death so I don't see why she should have it coming *and* going. It's my turn to go over the sticks. Go on, Mo, get in front with Roger. I'll be O.K. I don't suppose it'll be all that long till we get home.'

'You wait when we do,' the youth grated.

After all, she thought, if he wants to treat me as his property I may as well go in his boot like a suitcase.

The car jerked away at the thrust of his temper. The exhaust wafted in on her and with the wheels' bumpety-bump she knew what Maureen had gone through. It was like her life. That was just how ugly girls got treated. Still at least nobody wanted to have them like toys. Sheila did not know which was worse, to be somebody's or to be nobody's. Both as bad. Perhaps she would do Mo a good turn. She bobbed her head up and peered through the scratched square of perspex that formed the back window. She made out the two heads stiff as Belisha Beacons and quite mute. She bobbed down again, grinning to herself. It would be a real joke and teach Roger a lesson into the bargain. She could never understand why she was so perverse. I must be a bit tapped. Must ask Mum if it runs in the family. Any other girl'd be falling over herself to get her clutches on Roger Kelsall, but me—I have to go and spoil me chances every time. Why? Why? One answer she guessed. She intended sneaking off at the canal bridge. There would be other turns and other stops but none suited her so well.

They sped parallel with the cut now and the turning she was waiting for appeared. The car mounted the slope of the humpy bridge and stopped on the tilt ready to turn into the main road. Sheila slipped out of the boot and crept, well down, straight back and dodged behind a bush as the car made its turn and raced away.

Which way would it be? She hesitated, her thick brown hair tossing this way and that. Memory became instinct and guided her rightly. Chuckling, she fleeted along the towpath. Of course there wasn't the least chance of his being there, and even if he were, he would not be the same, would not remember her. Yet she had remembered him all these years. Seven or eight, was it? But what would she want now with a barge-lad? I'm daft, that's all there is to it. Under the bridges she saw her face in the water, a shadow, an echo, in her memory. She thought of the leeches swirling round the image and shivered and wondered how she could ever have wanted to catch them. Two boys were silently fishing. Ernie used always to be shushing her when they had lain like that, on their bellies. Turning to look back at the way she had come, she saw the tower of the asylum, stiff and red above parsley-like trees, and her feet slowed, leadened by she did not know what.

Fields lay back into woody hills on either side of her: this was the bargees' land as she had seen it years before. Still the same, only shrunk-looking. The barge-boy would

87

have left long since. Of course he would. He had gone already, the last time she came. But he might have come back. She tried to pretend to herself that he was not what she had come for.

Mossy scum and petals marbled the dead water. Few boats went up and down now. Many boatees were on the dole or lost among the townsfolk, busily forgetting their former life. A thrush beat a shell on stone and swallowed. Sheila caught the glinty relish in its eye as the beak dribbled. She remembered Judder's birds and his queer violence. Her heart thumped. She looked around. Every creature seemed intent on its own business: spiders trod at their threads; cows and horses and sheep cropped the grass, day-dreamily; bees and butterflies fleeced the buttercups and clover; a tandem dipped over the bridge ahead; white chickens finicked their fodder from the cakey earth; pigs lay flat out snoring; a man and a boy strode by with fishing baskets; water-rats plopped from their bank-holes; moor-hens skidded off to hide-outs in the reeds, and swans spruced their feathers as if to improve on perfection. It seemed strange to Sheila that she could feel glad at such general heedlessness of her.

She stopped. There it was, the chimney, the green roof of the boatees' cottage. And a barge lay lilting on the water beneath. Somebody was still there. Her heart seemed to rush ahead of her. Of course they wouldn't recognise her. And anyway, it wouldn't be them. She tiptoed forward, willing the event to be more exciting than it was. Then she swore aloud. Barbed wire and branches entwined to make a fence barring the pathway. She tried to climb it but fell back, panting and loosening her skirt from the barbs. She kicked the wire in temper.

Then she noticed a white-shirted figure leaning on a spade in a cabbage-patch watching her. She stepped back guiltily. He came stomping over to her. A bull-terrier also came and jumped at the fence with an officious bark and small proprietary eyes aflame.

'What the 'ell dost think thee't playin' at?'

Was it Judder? Could it be? If so, he was very different. The fair hair had darkened and was stringy with sweat and dirt. The face was square and stern, not too unlike; but the body was decidedly beefy, not a bit what she had expected. What *had* she expected? His blue-black eyes bore into her as if asking this very question. But the crude voice demanded,

'Wheer dost think the't gooin'?'

Her temper flared back. She was annoyed at her own mad ideas. Was this all she had come for? Who was he, any way, with his bloody common talk? Not Judder, plainly. Nostalgia was broken by the rough,

'How didst get 'ere?'

'By taxi—can't you see?'

He bent closer, over the barbs.

'Then thee'll t'ave goo back in it.'

'Why? This path is public.'

'Not now it inner.'

'Since when?'

'Since I put th'fence up.'

'You don't own the canal.'

'This stretch we do.'

'You can't own a path, you know.'

'Why can't I?'

'Don't be so daft.'

He felt like giving her a punch on the nose. But then he relaxed and scanned her. She lowered her eyes, colouring. There was a silence, save for a couple of motor-horns challenging each other far off.

'Look, clear off, wou't? Else I'll set Bonzo on thee.'

'Oh you will, will you? That's real fighting talk, I must say. That really scares me stiff.'

The dog was brawny and eager for action. She felt she might as well go home. But somehow she just wanted to make sure it was Judder. Or rather, wasn't. So she dashed the wire again with her foot. The youth rushed at her as if she were another man, not caring that he pushed her in the breast. Bonzo pranced up in hysterics and she was thrown back on the pathway. She felt half-stunned, more by his loutishness than the force of her fall. She lay and let herself cry a little, so that he stood idiotically staring at her, Bonzo trembling and whining to get his teeth in her. The youth gripped him by his collarless scruff and he subsided. Sheila wiped her eyes.

'You're a real fighting feller,' she sneered, slowly getting up.

He looked very sheepish and she laid on the pain of standing up. He unfastened the wire and gave a quick jerk of his head to beckon her through. As she passed him, her eyes flicked up and down him and she smiled into herself. There was *something* about him. She walked on past the peculiar cottage, throwing up a jaunty whistle as she went by the cabbages.

He watched her, nonplussed. The dog growled to leap after, but he caught it and stooped to let it lick his face. He pressed his nose into the hot hairy neck to get re-assurance. Girls scared him. He suspected they were different from men but didn't want to have to think so. His stomach had gone hollow when he saw her dumped on the ground by his blow. He grinned at the thought of what other lads said they had done with strange girls. Perhaps he should have dived on her and given her a good shagging. But he didn't want to. He watched the disappearing figure, wondering what it was men got out of what they said they did. He remembered a girl he had once got talking to in Congleton Market. But she knew nothing about anything except fustian-running, which was her job. He took her along the cut in his boat and tried to get her to play with him, but she was too worried about her father giving her a good hiding if he found out and every time she touched him she jumped out of her skin and spun round as if the world was watching. What he did not know was that she was on edge because she reckoned he should have been doing things to her, not she to him. So he never bothered with any more girls. He worked on the farm or the boats and he and Vincent looked after each other and the animals and needed nobody else. He went and ducked himself under the pump.

Sheila did not know what to do next. She was walking in the opposite direction to home. For God's sake, she said to herself, stopping suddenly and staring into a field of burnt grass, I came to see him, he's not here, so that's that. She felt fagged out. Judder had gone into nowhere. It was as if her own past had sunk into the earth. The day stretched far behind her like a whole hot history. She even wished she were back with Roger. Her eyes glazed and she sagged as she stared into the field. A couple of rabbits streaking the stubble brought her to herself. Like them she was just out to play. The rabbits set each other and darted together and then away just before they met. Talk about people, she laughed.

She wandered back, dragging her feet, glad of the evening breeze to unglue her flesh. Passing the cottage, she told herself she need not come again. The ghost was laid. Anyway she couldn't have gone out with a *boatee*. She peeped in at the door. The youth was standing wiping his wet head with a torn towel. Beyond him a strange large person sat in the shadows. Bonzo leapt forward and she dodged back. The youth came to the door, pushed the dog inside and shut it.

'Thee'st gor a cheek coming back 'ere.'

'Listen who's talking about cheek.'

He went shy. She knew there was nothing to be afraid of.

'I only thought——' She fixed his eyes brightly. He looked quite handsome now. 'I only thought somebody I once knew would be here.'

'Here?'

'A lad called Judder Chidlow. Did you know him?'

'What a't on about?'

Oh why am I standing here talking to *him*, she wondered, moving away. He made a supreme effort, not wanting her to go.

'Wheer dost come from?'

'Hanley. How long have you lived here?'

'Teow–threy years—on and off.'

'You're boatees?'

He nodded.

'He was a boatee.'

'Who?'

'This Judder I was telling you about.'

'Oh 'im.'

They did not know what to say next. Homing birds filled the air.

'What's up, Malky?' The door opened and a man's voice spoke out of the shadows within.

'Only this wench.'

'Tell her to eff off.'

The boy reddened.

'Eff off yourself,' Sheila called. So the lad's name was Malcolm. Pity.

'Dunna mind him,' Malcolm whispered. 'He inna well. He got gassed.'

'Gassed?'

'In th'war.'

'There's going to be another one,' she said, for no reason at all.

'Aah,' Malcolm nodded. 'That's right.'

They heard the other man coughing and spluttering fit to burst.

'He needs looking after,' the girl said.

'I look after him.' Malcolm became stern for a moment.

There was a slow shuffling and the man came to the door at last. Lit by the westering sun his face was quite a sight. It had a lumpy mauve stain all down one side. Sheila could not help stepping back. The man was enormous, but as if filled with air or water, not flesh. His trousers came up to the middle of his bow-fronted chest, which was bare save for wide braces. His body-skin was as smooth as a woman's, his chest like breasts.

'He canna stand th'eat,' Malcolm said, as if this explained everything .

Bonzo stood tremulously eyeing the scene from behind the wide flappy trousers.

The man spoke at last in his odd earth-fast sort of voice.

93

'What'st want? We dunna like bodies messing rind 'ere. It's private prop'ty. So mess off with yer.'

'It's O.K., Vincent. 'Er's just going.'

'But I've only just come,' Sheila objected. 'I'm not going back just like that.'

'Look.' Vincent jerked his purpled head. 'Bugger off.'

'I shan't. Not unless he takes me.'

She plonked herself down on the grass.

An urgent whispering started up between the two men. Sheila speculated idly whether they were planning to kidnap her. Supposing Vincent, and not Malcolm, raped her? But it seemed highly unlikely that either would, they were too simple and bewildered and kept scratching their heads and tugging their ear-lobes. Vincent began to nod and his breasts wobbled as Malcolm murmured on at him. Malcolm then came towards her.

'Come on.'

He's making progress, she thought. Pity I shan't see him again. Might have got somewhere. She followed him eagerly into the barge.

'Shall I be safe?' she giggled, glancing back at Vincent, who gazed expressionlessly after her.

'Safe?' Malcolm hadn't a clue what she was getting at. 'It dunna leak.'

'I was only joking.'

Vincent watched them float through the calm air. He stood like a statue.

They chugged into the down-spreading sun. The years might never have happened: familiar scenes unfolded backwards like time itself. They moved from the shaved cornfields and September woods into the scrubland of long khaki grass, touched by neither man nor beast but only dust and smoke. The pit-heaps and humping lanes of pubs and pot-banks starkened in the pink and gold. At last, starting with Ownshaw's Sports Ground, came the stretch of cut that had once been Sheila's and Ernie's special haunt. But she could never regret being a child no more.

'Shall you come this way again p'raps?'

She looked up in surprise. She had not reckoned on him saying this but was glad he showed a hint of normality. He had said nothing during the journey, but occasionally he had looked thoughtfully at her thoughtful face.

'Could do.' She shrugged, sure that she felt nothing. It would be something different, something to be going on with now that Roger was done with—though she hadn't known until this moment that Roger *was* done with. It might as well be Malcolm as anybody, though she wished to God that wasn't his name.

'When then?'

'Soonish.'

'When's that?'

She sighed, resenting commitment as usual.

'Wednesday—p'raps—I'm not really——'

'I'll be waiting 'ere.' They were at the steps to her street. 'Thee'lt be by theeself, mind, wusna?'

'O.K. Just me.'

'What time?'

'Oh,' she shrugged. 'After tea. T'ra. Thanks for the ride.'

'I'll be 'ere then.'

He didn't know how he managed to sound so casual, since he had gone all of a quiver inside. Whatever was he doing? Vincent would have a fit. He didn't know whether he dared expect her or whether he wanted her even, but he was exultant as he watched his boat divide the gnats on the gleaming water. Though he dared not look back, he sensed somehow that she was peeping over the parapet of the bridge watching him go. But when he could no longer resist turning his head to see, she was not there after all.

X

It was crazy really. He was nothing but a yokel. Here she was getting dolled up and baby-powdered, and he would probably smell like a cowshed. She would peep over the bridge and there he would be. What kids we all are. Worse than kids—I was never like this as a kid.

The streets were alive with children playing under the flawless sky. Sheila made her way through them, helloing here and there, being gaped at, sure of what she was but not sure what she wanted.

Malcolm was not there. All assurance fell from her. What did she expect? What did it matter? It mattered. She dashed a fair way along the canal-side before she saw his boat chugging forward. She opened her mouth to call, then shut it. Why should I chase him? But it opened again in spite of her. He started at the shout and looked round in alarm. He had sped away relieved as soon as he saw that she was not there. He had dreaded the meeting all day, the thought of what he must do and say, the business of getting spruced up, the impossibility of it all. He had stopped and nearly turned back half a dozen times, but his dog gazed at him as if he was daft so he went on. It had been the answer to his prayer, not finding her at the bridge. But there was a roused stranger in him, too, that wanted her very much to be there. He resented this new self, wishing to enjoy the evening in his own usual way, just to chug along alone and unhampered, and do a bit of fishing. Now it was as if the

97

cut was thick with reeds that baulked his progress. The girl was going to be a nuisance. He contemplated her, half-minded to get going and leave her where she was, waving and smiling uncertainly on the footpath. But the lift of her slim colourful figure from the black earth drew at him and made him long for something he could not put a name to. With a fate-accepting sigh he stopped the engine and waited whilst she came up to him. She was furious with herself for showing so willing but she couldn't help it.

'You don't wait long for anybody, do you?'

'I didna think thee'dst come.'

'You mean you hoped I wouldn't.'

He did not contradict her.

'Aren't you going to let me on your precious boat then?'

He slid the brass bar back but he did not put an arm out to help her. She jumped in, watched suspiciously by Bonzo. Her heel twisted inelegantly and, looking for somewhere to sit and regain her dignity, she hovered her bottom on to a heaped tarpaulin and peered self-consciously about her. Malcolm's arms hung limp and he seemed not to know what to do with her now that she was there. A kiln-man came for coolness out of Ownshaw's pot-bank and sat on a crate of ware, whistling *Twas on the Isle of Capri*. He got out his pipe and tried to light it in the misting air, flicking match after match into the cut before Sheila's and Malcolm's mesmerised eyes. The man looked as though he was deliberately try-ing not to question the silence and motionlessness of the pair, accepting their presence as a fixture of the scene along with black bottle-ovens and white clay-hills. He held his pipe in his mouth unlit. The boy and girl stared at each other, hardly seeming to breathe at all, caught in a suspense that came from his fear and her puzzlement.

'Aren't we going to go?' She broke the spell.

'Aah.' A nervous joy plucked his hands to the engine and the barge drew forward, to the relief of the kiln-man who was able to light his pipe at last.

Malcolm scanned straight ahead the now bright now dark water. What must I do with her? She could not see his panic, only a self-contained speechless mystery. What's he after? Suppose he takes me into the bushes. Suppose he's batty like his friend? He might even do me in or something. She kept a long nail file at the ready in case of emergency and she looked to make sure it was in her bag. She casually extracted a packet of cork-tipped fags and offered him one.

'No ta, I dunna smeowk.'

'No vices I see.'

He did not know how to respond to banter and simply looked red and shy. Sheila shrugged to herself and they were mute again. Oh God, I'm in for a right evening with him. Perhaps I shouldn't have given Roger the push after all. She felt herself urging from the tarpaulin as if to speed the boat on, but they glided in the same even serenity, just coming into greenness beyond the aluminium works. She felt again the strangeness of the familiar world when it was viewed from on the water. Scenes from her life went by like a slow-motion film. The pit-heaps were pyramids black on the spun sky; the shanks of the poor town spindled to a hilltop; a scrubby farm of not-very-green fields and not-very-clean cows sprouted a hedging of advertisements; and in the basin-bottom of the valley sewage works unloosed their ulti-mate smell almost solid-seeming against the static air.

Fancy me doing this all over again. It was a backward move, recovering things she had determined should have no further place in her life. She glanced at the heavy figure in its half-pressed cream shirt and mealy flannels. Why doesn't he speak? He mustn't ever have taken a girl out before. And now he's got me. *Me*. Some men'd give I don't know what.

'I put another fella off for you tonight, you know.'

He swerved his eyes down to study his feet. What's she after? Why did she pick on me?

'He'd've taken me out in his car—sports model.'

'Where'd he have taken thee then?'

'Oh—to a pub in the country. Somewhere posh.'

'I know a pub.' He was showing life at last.

Thank God, she sighed to herself. Else I thought we'd sit here all night and say nowt.

He had a purpose now and seemed very changed, lit with a bright forward-pointing smile. As she sat in front of him she merged with the horizon and became the same point which he was making for.

'Where is this pub then?'

'At Consall forge. Not fur now.'

He managed the locks and his boat so deftly she did not notice how far they had gone.

'Chidlow Gulch is up there,' she said, happily surprised.

He looked up inquiringly.

'But you wouldn't know,' she said. 'It was only what he called it.'

'That Judder you were telling me about?'

She nodded. If only he were Judder.

'He made me cry there.'

Malcolm gazed sorrowfully at her. He could hardly

imagine her crying. She smiled to herself. His question-
ing look was like a dog's, though not *his* dog's. *His* dog
lay pretending to be asleep, and occasionally its pinkish
impersonal eye would open to make sure she was
behaving herself.

'Haven't you got any parents?'

The asylum tower had come into view.

'Oh ah. Me mam and me uncle.'

'Your uncle?'

'Me mam got married again soon as me dad popped
off.'

'Is that why you took up with Vincent?'

He nodded brightly, she grimly.

'Vincent's been good to me—got me a job on eowd
Simcox's so I dunna 'ave to rely on th'boat. Boating's not
what it was, thee knowst.'

'Yes, I know.'

Nothing was what it had been.

The pub was across the railway-track that ran beside
the cut, and opposite a toy-like station. It was just
a tumbledown back cottage, not a bit like Roger's
Cunarder-style place. There was no road to it, only
a cart-track linking station and forge. There were no
spanking sports cars parked outside, only an old van and
two ponies and traps, whips neatly curled across their
fronts. The ponies' faces muzzled together in the quietest
of conversations. Most of the customers had come on foot,
being labourers from red-grey farms or the new paper-
mill. Hens pecked everywhere and grubby dogs barked
and were answered by Bonzo and shouted at from within
doors. Sheila felt displaced from her own time as if in a
world not on any map. She wished Roger were there.
The gloomy-beamed place was chock full of beery men

who gave her wet idiot-looks as she sauntered in, her eyes flickering round to ensure that she was the focus of attention. She need not have bothered; the silent faces jutted full of expectation. Then the talk was resumed, self-consciously loud and assured.

'Aren't you going to ask me what I'll have, then?' the girl glinted at Malcolm's dithering.

'Oh—yes—sit you down somewheer.'

Roger would have led her to the quietest corner of the most select room and asked,

'Is it the usual?'

But there was no quiet corner and no select room, only the spit-and-sawdust.

'Gin and it then. Go on. They'll know what it is.'

Even if you don't, you dope, she added under her breath.

He couldn't get the words out quickly enough when he reached the bar again. He didn't want the other men to hear. But they all did and they smirked and nudged one another because he said it as if reading from a black-board. The old-lady bar-tender muttered against every ordinary order, let alone an extravagance such as this.

'Gin and it. Gin and it. Whatever next?'

But she knew what it was and was pleased at having to do something new and important. She stooped under the bar, and, peering up at Malcolm over it, reached for a sherry-glass. She creaked up and placed the glass on the counter, smiling a two-toothed smile, her eyes seeming turned inside out in the strangeness of the effort. She was just about to pour in the gin when Malcolm shifted the glass.

'Its' got dust on,' he forced himself to object, sweating so freely his thumb-marks greased the dust. The old

102

woman tutted and wiped the glass on her dirty pinafore, still cocking a humorous white eye at the lad.

'Dust, he says, *dust.*'

She did her special performance again, scrupulous about measures yet still managing to hold Malcolm in the twist of her gaze. Why the heck does she take so long, he squirmed.

At last he lurched off with his tiny tray on which the little glass clinked against his pint mug. This has happened before, Sheila suddenly told herself. I've done this before. She sat up and looked around. Blotchily bronzed faces leered at her.

'You certainly see life in the country, I must say.'

She spoke loudly, conscious of being listened to as one distinguished and sophisticated. The drinkers felt their lives approved of and one of them winked at her. Sarcasm was lost on them as on Malcolm, who was beginning to look too pleased with himself. Don't say he's getting like Roger already, she thought. Have I got to show him I'm not *his* prize possession too? She got up and made for the bar. She had bought cigarettes and the second round before he knew what she was doing.

'These're on me.' She turned to meet his hot face as he came up to the bar behind her, his hands foolishly outstretched.

'No, they anna.'

'Yes, they are. I've paid—see.'

The old woman gave her change and again smiled her dry smile at Malcolm as she did so. He looked fiercely at Sheila and she touched his lapel.

'Dunna make a fuss, there's a good lad.'

He wanted to punch her and get her down under him. She guessed what was going on behind his angry eyes and thought to herself, 'Oh, aren't I awful?' She lit a cigarette and blew smoke into his face as if she were Barbara Stanwyck. He could not bear her hunching over her lighter or the ecstasy of her first puff.

'What dost 'ave smeowk fer?'

She beckoned as if she was going to let him in on a secret. He bent his head expectantly. Her smoke went with her whisper into his ear,

'I like to smoke—that's what for.'

Then she pushed his nose with her forefinger-end.

'Oh 'eck.' He shot up.

'Whatever's the matter?'

'It's gone dark. We shonna be able goo back in th' boat.'

'P'raps we could sleep in it,' she suggested with an odd laugh.

'No fear,' he replied disconcertingly. 'Vincent'd get worried.'

'Sounds as though Vincent's the most important person in your life.'

'Yes,' he said simply. 'That's right.'

He moved off to speak to a pimpled youth at the darts board.

Well, I like that, she thought, it isn't natural, men being like that about each other. The pimpled youth glanced across at her as Malcolm spoke to him, and she looked down her nose, not caring greatly for her new boy-friend's world.

'Eric's goin' take us far as our 'ouse. Then we can wowk th' rest.'

They went to Eric's mother's cottage where his van was parked, at the long lane's end. Sheila shivered, sensing but not seeing swift motion: September wind in the trees, bats sailing the black air, and the weir's rush. It was not her world at all, nor one she had credited the existence of, so closed in on itself. It was made stranger still by a glow-worm at the path's edge. She had never seen one before and the green luminosity seemed almost a trick to her. But it was as familiar to Malcolm as the street-lamps outside her home were to her. He laughed at her amazement, exulting that she was the ignorant and baffled one for once. Looking at the curl of un-earthly light, she did not know where she was.

The drive in Eric's van lay along a woodland path so narrow the trees met above their passing, moths and leaves fluttering for a moment's individuality into the head-lamps and back into blackness. Sheila sat in front with Eric while Malcolm and Bonzo lay spread out in the back among sacks and pitchforks. He could not take his eyes from the silhouette of the girl's face with its smouldering dot of a fag gliding up and down and glow-ing more brightly now and then to the suck of her breath.

When they got out and said goodnight to Eric, Malcolm peeped in at the cottage to make sure Vincent was asleep and to leave Bonzo on guard. Sheila hid as bidden behind the door, jumping at the scufflings that came out of the night. Then the young couple made their way carefully along the tow-path. Malcolm knew every step and took Sheila's hand from time to time for the rough bits, but dropped it as soon as these were passed. She sensed the onset of the town by the change of smell from a heathery to a sewagey one. She was glad, however, to see the lights and the traffic and to come on to known ground.

Now he wanted to get away from her. He needed to stand back from what had happened and think about it before going any further. So he let her go at the end of her street, without the hint of a kiss. She even pressed near him and made her voice dreamy and her body floppy—just to see. But all he said was,

'I'll fetch th'boat back termorrer.'

'I see.'

'Er——'

'Yes?'

'We can meet Friday if thee want'st.'

'Do *you* want?'

There was a pause during which he made enormous efforts, culminating in,

'Do *you* want?'

'I asked you first.'

'Yes,' he said with a silly embarrassed laugh and she didn't know what he was agreeing to.

'All right then.'

Well, she thought, as she turned indoors, he's a bit of a goof, but perhaps I can make something of him.

She did not know that he bounded back along the towpath, stepping surely, leap-frogging stiles and zig-zagging in every field till he sank puffed out at last into the buttercups and bruised clover.

Looking up at the stars he recalled his first meeting with Vincent along the one-track railway. Malcolm was out of work and spending his time fishing. Vincent went by each day, with his bull-terrier at his heels, checking the rails. They got talking and Malcolm never minded about the lumpy mauve face. He got to know all about the trenches in the war and other things as well. Vincent had a quiet way of ordering life that drew Malcolm to him. He had only to snap his fingers and Bonzo would do whatever was wanted of him. It was Vincent who persuaded old Simcox that he needed another hand on the farm and Malcolm was taken on. From then on Malcolm and Vincent had their breakfasts and mid-day meals together. When he had finished checking a stretch of rail, Vincent would come with his knapsack and join the youth under a hay-rick. On cold or wet days they shifted to a hut along the railway line and sat eating their cheese among oil-cans and spanners. Malcolm had never known such cosiness, for his parents' home was not a happy one. The two men would sit munching contemplatively. When Vincent roused himself to speak he did so from the smoky fathoms of his hand-rolled cigarettes, and he usually spoke about his experience of war, making Malcolm strangely glad that people sometimes spoke of another one coming. Vincent had been all over the world, to hear him talk, and it seemed weird that the quiet man pacing the same stretch of track day in day out should contain in himself faraway places and long-ago battles. But most of the stories were of women, women he had known, one way and another, before he got gassed. Malcolm always guessed when a great revelation was coming, as it would be preceded by Vincent's putting his hands in his corduroy trouser pocket and settling his privates into a more comfortable position. He must have had a hole in his pocket, too, as sometimes he would sniff fastidiously at his fingers.

'Aah,' he would say tonelessly, 'I've seyn just abite ow there is t'be seyn. Thee'dst bey surprised what people get up to in different parts. I've seyn young bits of girls —ten, twelve yeer na mower, with little Arab lads with whoppers this long.'

He placed his hand at least eighteen inches from his trouser front.

'No kiddin'. You wouldna thowt thee'd a rad cocks any bigger than Woodbines, even on the 'onk, but I tell thee I've seyn 'em with me own eyes. Thee must get plenty a rexercise, that's ow thee is t'be said abite it.'

Malcolm tittered, uncertain what response was called for and thinking there must in fact be quite a lot more to be said about it. But Vincent remained poker-faced, save that he pointed two fingers forward in the form of a pistol, lifted his behind and solemnly broke wind. Then he sniffed, swallowed and spat and went on rummaging in his memories and his trouser-pocket.

'There's wenches in Egypt'll go with anythink, man or beast, niggers and camels and God knows what. Wey kneow nite in this country, nite I tell thee. Thee'lt sey it ow fer theesen. Thee's nite like it fer seyin' th'wonders of th'world.'

From that day on Malcolm looked forward to these wonders and never reckoned on finding them under his nose.

When his father died and his mother married his Uncle Percy and went to live in Cheadle, Vincent got old Simcox to let him and Malcolm have the bargee's cottage by the canal. The pair bought a boat between them, and they were happy.

But now this had happened, this Sheila had come, and Malcolm didn't know what he wanted any more. He picked himself up from the dewy earth and, both elated and depressed, strode on into the fragrant darkness.

There was a light in the cottage window and Malcolm heard Bonzo's bark of dry welcome. Vincent had lit the lamp and sat up waiting in his night-shirt, a newly rolled cigarette between his fingers. Malcolm palpitated slightly as he entered. Neither man spoke for a few minutes. Then,

'Nice bit of stuff.' Vincent lit up at last.

Malcolm nodded, grinning with relief.

'Thee'lt 'ave be careful though, Malky.'

The boy's head jerked enquiringly. Vincent got into bed, still smoking.

'I bet 'er kneows a thing or teow. I bet 'er's 'ad bagsa rexperience. And 'er'll be looking for satisfaction, thee knowst. 'Er'll mess thee abite. 'Er'll want things different from what thee are. Men dunna like women's wees and women dunna like men's and thee's no gerrin' rind it. Thee're fidget-arses. Thee'st berrer off it thee cost deow withite 'em, but sometimes thee cosna and that's thee dinefow.'

'Dunna worry about mey,' Malcolm said, sitting on the older man's bed to take off his boots and trousers before he got into his own. Vincent dropped his fag-end into a jerry, where it sizzled among his spit. Then, with his outstretched hand, he carefully felt at the youth's' privates.

'Just seeing if thee'st got whar it takes,' he murmured, very seriously.

Malcolm did not mind, but he felt empty and he was sorry for Vincent because his life was all behind him and the war had laid him waste. I shan't let that happen to me, he thought. And when Vincent had one of his coughing bouts because of the cigarette he had smoked, Malcolm got him a glass of water and soothed his fiery head back on to the pillow.

XI

If only autumn were not coming on, Liddy thought. It seemed the end of things. Yet life should have just been beginning for her. There hadn't been much to it up to now. It had always lined the horizon, something she expected to be released into it at any moment, and she could not help thinking now that Clive was helping to hold her back. He was more than ever like a big loving dog, happy at every sight and sound and smell. He was more complete—it seemed funny to say so—than she was. Simply being himself, with the world going on around him, was enough. It should have been all she wanted, to be with him. But she wanted something more, somebody else. All there was was an old man. So Mrs. Hordell called him, and

'I can tell you what he's after,' she said.

Mr. Cahill was a widower in his fifties and he kept the local chemist's shop. Liddy had gone there to get something for her period pains.

He peered over his bottles at her, like something out of a Disney cartoon, seeming to grow taller every minute, a wizardy smile on his rimless-spectacled face as he mixed concoctions and counted out pills. When he brought them to her, he said,

'It's all in the mind, Miss Slater. You don't really need these things at all.'

As if he possessed her inmost secrets and knew her better than she did herself. She responded to anything that seemed likely to change the pattern of her existence that had been laid down without any reference to her wishes. She did not want marriage, since that choice seemed to put an end to all others and gave only one road to go on. She learned to like older men for want of better, even ones whose pewtery tweeds reeked of cough mixture. There was much power in Mr. Cahill's straight still body and meticulous hands and his eyes that always seemed to be smiling at something just behind her head. Her blushes in the darkness of the car when he said, after their first evening out together,

'You've been lovely tonight, really lovely,' were of pleasure as much as embarrassment. She did not resist his kiss, though his moustache tickled her nose into a violent sneeze. And while the smell of wine failed to cover that of some disinfectant that he habitually breathed from his well-kept teeth, the kiss seemed a token of what she had missed in having no father, and she cried at tiny possibilities of fulfilment unfolding like daisies.

Shopkeepers had been threatening powers behind her mother's life, though Doris had rarely acknowledged them. So a shop seemed to the girl the essence of security, and to this one she was drawn more and more often. Through a baize door or behind bead curtains lurked cosy mysteries. Mr. Cahill's apartments were upstairs. Mounting, Liddy felt both a sense of privilege and a shiver of fear. The shop had just closed one afternoon, and the apothecary had let down the blinds over the coloured bottles, leaving a shaft of sun on the fake-marble floor.

'Come and have a cup of tea,' he suggested, 'I can check the till later.'

She would dearly have liked to check the till with him.

'Did Mrs. Cahill do the till for you?'

'Oh no. Mrs. Cahill was a lady.'

The girl did not know what to say. She looked at all the photographs of Mrs. Cahill on the piano. She had been taken in various unflattering poses and was often badly tinted.

'Oh yes,' Liddy faltered as if she should have seen straightaway what Mrs. Cahill was.

He smiled curiously at her, and she did not know what expression she should put on. She was as terrified of misinterpreting as of being misinterpreted.

'Shall I put the kettle on?' She made a bid for safety.

'Wait a bit. I want to show you something.'

She suppressed her imaginings, even though he guided her into his bedroom. Deliberately studying the furniture for dust and disappointed to find none, she tried hard not to shrink back from the double bed that had two pillows on it. His eyes glintingly followed hers.

'I always lay a place for Mrs. Cahill.'

'That's very nice of you.' Her flesh went goose-pimply. She caught sight of herself in the dressing-table mirror, where the scene appeared like one on a film-screen.

'This is it.' He opened the wardrobe door.

Mrs. Cahill's dresses, coats and suits hung like a history of twentieth-century costume.

'You can have the lot.'

He plainly thought he was bestowing treasures. Liddy gaped, impressions crowding in on her. Amid them she could already hear Mrs. Hordell's caustic remarks. The chemist took out a flouncy purple dress.

'Try it on. Go on, don't be shy.'

She stood limp and dispirited.

'I'll leave you to it. Whilst I put the kettle on.'

He smiled and motioned her to the wardrobe.

'Go on. Help yourself.'

She tried to smile back and stood like a dummy till he left the room. Then she turned to the dressing-table mirror.

'What is it? What is it he wants?'

But she knew the real question was, what do I want? He was sure of himself while she was sure of nothing. The kettle's whistle sent her hurrying to snatch a brown and white crepe dress with clasps in the form of yellow butterflies. It was too short and too loose, for Mrs. Cahill had been a small fat body. But in the effort of making herself presentable Liddy grew engrossed and tried on a fur jacket and a wide-brimmed hat also butterfly patterned. She meant to take the jacket and hat off before presenting herself to Mr. Cahill, but he knocked at the door and she said 'Come in' before she knew what she was doing.

'Ah.' He cocked his head on one side appreciatively. 'Tea is served, madam.'

She looked round as if there was somebody else there. But it was herself whom he ushered, a napkin over his arm, to the glittering tea-table. Silver-dotted cakes stood on the silver tiers of the cake-stand. She was about to put off her hat when he said,

'Oh, no. Don't remove it. It goes with your ginger hair. From now on I'd like to call you Ginger. May I?'

'I'm not a bit like Ginger Rogers.'

'That's not the point.'

She smiled perplexedly and glanced round for her cup,

feeling very silly, sitting like somebody in a café and wearing clothes that neither suited nor fitted her. She was hard put to it, too, to keep her skirt over her suspenders. It was like some shaming dream, or a German film, yet she strangely enjoyed it, because for the first time in her life somebody was making a real fuss of her.

Suppose he thinks I'm her, though. Suppose he forgets who I am. She was annoyed at her own amenability, feeling like one of the chemical mixtures poured into the test-tube of Mrs. Cahill's clothes, smooth and uncharactered. She longed to burst out with her own self, yet she never could, here or anywhere. She felt that all her true features faced inwards and only the wrong side, like a potting mould, turned to the outside world. It seemed awful that it was this crude outside that Mr. Cahill was taken with, and that he did not bother to look for the real thing. But then what did she see of him save his queer smile and white-dusted moustache and pernickety hands? What did they tell her about all that he thought, all that he was to himself? She wondered whether Mrs. Cahill had ever come to know his underside. Liddy did not even know what was under his shirt and trousers and she kept her imagination in check. It was not for girls to speculate about men's bodies as men did about girls'. Specially old men's bodies. It was funny, though, the thought did not sicken her. No, it did not sicken her. She would have liked to see. Men were supposed to mentally undress girls, and he had done the exact opposite. But what if he meant to undress her after tea, and what if he expected to find his wife's body underneath? Stop it, she said to herself.

'I don't suppose Mrs. Cahill wore her fur cape for tea at home.'

'No, but you're not at home, are you?'

She flushed, realising she couldn't say yes or no to this. Did he not like her to speak of his wife?

'How's your brother keeping now?'

She could not tell whether he asked this to cover her confusion or by way of retaliating.

'Not so bad. Only thing is, they're looking after him too well. He's getting fat.'

'That does happen in such cases. Then they don't last long. It's a blessing really.'

She looked stricken because he had expressed her own thought, but he assumed he had been insensitive and he coughed. There was silence. Suddenly he leaned forward, upsetting his cup.

'It's a damn shame such children have to be born.'

'Yes.' It was a relief to hear someone else say it.

'They've stopped it in Germany.'

For a moment Liddy wildly thought he meant all sexual intercourse.

'That's one thing you've got to give old Adolf—he's scientific and no messing.'

Liddy didn't know where to look, he was so intense and his brow gleamed. *He* might have been the one with the idiot brother.

'You wouldn't like to have children like that, would you?' he asked urgently. 'You of all people.'

She shook her head, but rebelled inwardly against this singling out. A vein throbbed in the man's head. He frightened her: though he voiced her own feelings about daft children, he did so in a way that made them seem shocking. She felt awe of him, as at something beyond her. The air of the room was alive with it. Suppose he decided to do her in so that she *couldn't* have such children. Perhaps he was a sort of Doctor Crippen. She reminded herself sharply that Mrs. Cahill had died in hospital, after an operation. But suppose he had mutilated her first. Stop it at once, she said almost out loud. He looked questioningly at her and, as the intensity passed from his eyes, there came something even appealing in them.

Changing her clothes thankfully in the bedroom she was disturbed at herself more than at him, knowing that if he had cared to try anything she would have given in. Just like her mother. She looked at the lace curtains fluttering at the bottom of the open sash and then up at the white clouds that crept over the black slates and worn-crowned chimneys.

As she was let out of the house, saying her thank-you, the inevitability of so many things drained her. She was ganted so little will of her own, there might as well be none. She was a prisoner of the streets and a grey life. She recalled her school-leaving day when the Headmistress told the girls to value their independence. But in this first, last and switched-on intimacy she had neglected to explain what independence meant. Nothing surely to girls who had to find jobs and needed love. Or was it what one gave up for these?

It was not hard to give up what she had never really had. She became glad of Mr. Cahill's ever-presence at her elbow. Perhaps he was her destiny. Another stupid word, meaning merely the shabbiness of doing what she had to do in the usual unexciting way. Like visiting Clive. Once she admitted she was fed up with it, it became easier to go on. She had wasted energy forcing her feelings in the wrong direction. When he died, it was as if her resentment had become a wish granted.

'You get what you want but not the way you want it,' was a favourite saying of Mrs. Hordell's, and now Liddy saw that this was true. Clive had simply plonked himself down on the refectory floor one day, grown redder and redder and fit to burst like a pig's bladder. As when her mother died, Liddy felt she should have known by telepathy the moment of his passing. But she was at the pictures with Mr. Cahill at the time. And it was he who saw her through the bereavement, managing the undertakers and the insurance policies, providing her with Mrs. Cahill's Persian lamb coat because she had no black of her own and, above all, convincing her that it was all for the best. When she had thought so herself, it seemed like the whispering of guilt, but when he said it it seemed scientifically true, even though, unlike most people she saw around her, Clive had enjoyed life so much.

Mr. Cahill, of course, decided on cremation as something modern, clean and thorough. At first Liddy shuddered at such sudden nothingness. In earth the lad would still be there like roots of a felled tree. But then she saw how good it would be to rid him of the body that had dragged him in its grossness. She stood poised over it, wishing she could dissolve it with a glance and have him in the air about her. He smelt sweeter now than he had ever done in life. Nor did he look so cretinous, but simply like some old fat animal, bear or badger, taken by age and content to be so. Once again she envied him. Perhaps he had even enjoyed his dying. She wouldn't put it past him. How odd that he should be dropped into flames just as the first cold October days were coming. Not that he ever felt the cold, being in a constant lather. The funeral was too bland and clean and thin, unsuited to him. Three cars passed like slugs between the new crematorium lawns which were edged with melancholy Michaelmas daisies. The distempered chapel was like a hospital ward, save that the chrysanthemums were in the form of wreaths. The dealwood coffin was filled with the whiteness of corpse and shroud. If only, Liddy thought, it were the last day and he could rise and take back his life, changed and made knowing. But not here, not now, not in this dry all-electric nothingness. Ernie was playing muffled hymns on the electronic organ and the service passed like a dream, an identical dream for each box that passed through the blue velvet curtains into the furnace whose heat underlay the chapel, making the air like cotton wool and the mourners sweat into their blanketing black. Only the air seemed solid; all else was ghostly. If only the fire would rise and swallow them all, along with the coffin that bumped its way on the conveyor belt, as if with Clive's own clumsiness, into what the stokers called the back of beyond.

'Bodies sit up in the fire,' Mrs. Hordell muttered to her friend Mrs. Fetchford as, connoisseurs of death, they filed out of the chapel to Ernie's soft glossy music. 'So Corny Hilditch says, and he should know. They twitch.'

'I can well believe it,' Mrs. Fetchford replied mysteriously, loosening her top teeth and letting them crash inside her mouth. She had been wondering, as she always did, how much longer she had got to go, being nearly ninety now.

Round about them people were saying the usual hopeless things.

'It's a blessing.'

'——better off out of the way.'

'Good job they dunna last long.'

As if they had superior inklings of the meaning of life. Some discussed the various funeral methods open to them all.

'I suppose it's the best thing really, but it inner very nice.'

'At least you'd know you were properly dead.'

'Fancy weeking up undergrind kneowng as thee cosna ger ite.'

Mr. Cahill drew Liddy out of hearing, but she did not mind what the voices said. It was happening to Clive now, but it would happen to them all soon. He was different from them in life, but they would be the same as him in death. They talked about it to bring it into the ordinariness of everything else they did.

XII

The war began and Sheila went on munitions which meant getting up in the dark and setting off up the frost-and-torch-twinkly street for the special utility bus that seemed springless. The ROF workers were so far mainly men and she had a job keeping them off even in the dun dawn-light, for, as one girl acidly said, 'People only come on munitions to get snifters.' They all stood in a small shuffling queue outside the Palace cinema looking, as the sky cracked open, like a set of spotted dumplings.

The bus sped miles out into the countryside beyond Selham Park. In fact it was allowed to drive through the grounds because of the emergency. Sheila wondered why anybody had bothered to wait for the war to begin, since they seemed to have known for ages that it was going to happen. Perhaps 'they' had agreed on a starting-time, just as her father said they had. Everyone wanted to believe that an early date was likewise appointed for the game to end. But one morning a murmur went round the bus that the Selham deer had gone. Sheila was filled with dread. This seemed to be it. She had loved to see them, heavenly in the mist, fleeting from the bus's dead rattle. Nobody knew what had become of them. One man said they had been taken to Scotland, another that they had been shot and tinned ready for the troops when they mobilised. They were gradually replaced, along with many trees ripped from their places on the eighteenth century architect's plan, by a grid of Nissen huts. For refugees, it was said. For prisoners-of-war. For V.I.P.s to hatch plans in. One taciturn woman said, with a set face.

'It's a concentration camp. You'll see.'

Few knew then what this meant, but whatever the huts were for, they blighted the pleasure-park.

It was the same with the Ordnance Factory, set slap in the middle of somebody's farm, so that when the workers stepped out of the canteen they gazed over miles of furrows and turnip-tops instead of the market-square or the canal. The interminable corrugations of roofs were being painted with mud-coloured waves as if, and oddly it turned out to be so, to create an optical illusion. Sheila came to enjoy the quietness of the country-side as a relief from belts and lathes whizzing and pounding. Even the smells of cabbages and manure were welcome after oil and explosive fumes. Her sleep was filled with the shapes of bullets, grenades, and bombs. There were endless smutty tales passed around. When one girl confessed that she had dreamt of a shell 'shooting up me fanny', the others wore stange gleaming smiles like snakes as they listened. And when they saw their handiwork stacked in millions of cases being rushed away by truck and train, the workers wondered where it could all be going to. There seemed enough to kill the whole world.

In this accepted hell of dull metal and sulphurous warmth, where tannoy voices grated through the greasy clangour, Sheila's hands worked like goblins, as if without any direction from her brain. She was forever turning over what Malcolm had said to her the evening before, or rather, because that was always so little, the way he had said it.

As for him, he would pause after swinging his tractor round at the edge of a field and look vacantly at his tracks where crows and jackdaws, with the occasional sea-gull, strutted and snatched about. He would seem to see the girl smiling from the dark red mouths of earth, that typical smile which rendered him tiny and helpless. He wanted to crush it into him. But she was the one who started things off. He just stood there waiting.

One evening he led her to a hill-top overlooking Leek. The silk mills reared like Italian palaces out of the dark moors and poked their chimney towers into the ribs of the Roches, familiars now of Sheila. Dying heather poured melancholy indigo to every horizon save the lit west where it was sea-green. Sheila felt very hollow. It was the right moment for love, but nothing was happening. She would not take his hand. Her first move was to get him to notice Roger's ring which she had deliberately put on. She kept pointing at things and asking what they were, fluttering her fingers as she did so, but Malcolm answered patiently and didn't twig. So she suddenly gave a yelp and hid her hands behind her back.

'What's up?'

'Oh nothing.' She squirmed theatrically.

'What'st got theer?'

'Nothing.'

'Let's see.'

They danced round each other, he trying to prise her fingers open, she trying to get him into the right position so that he would be pressed against her front with his arms round her waist. But instead of that he went the most direct way about it and twisted her arm so roughly she gave a genuine squeak and surrendered the ring, surprised, annoyed, and unkissed.

'You've hurt me,' she was glad to be able to say.

He ignored her and looked at the ring, baffled as usual. It hadn't seemed to be worth the trouble.

'Did a lad give it thee?'

'What d'you think? Wish I'd kept on with him and not gone out with you. *He* never twisted my arm out of its socket.'

'Why didsna keep on with him then?'

She shrugged. He handed her the ring.

'It's none of your business,' she said.

He turned away, looking hopelessly into the sunset. Then, 'Of course it's your business, you bloody fool,' she almost yelled at him. 'Don't you care if I'm somebody else's girl? Don't you want to kiss me—*ever?*'

She went for him then and bumped her lips on his. When they stood apart she thought he was going to run away, so she grabbed him, saying,

'This way, duck.' She wrapped his arms round her and lay into him.

It was as if kissing was the latest invention. From then on he liked best to be snuffling and close, the world shut out. It was like being right inside himself but not alone there any more. The only bit he didn't like was the fag-sourness sometimes on her breath, his own being grassy like a cow's. She often grew bored with his pawing and footsying. Sometimes his arm seemed like a boa-constrictor on her shoulders. She would wriggle from it, unwilling to make the relationship seem permanent. The trouble was, she was sometimes struck by the depth of her taste, and she never introduced him to her friends. Her mother only saw him once and when she did, she said,

'Good God girl, what d'you want go mashing with a cow'and for?'

'What's it matter,' Sheila shrugged, 'now there's a war on?'

But several times she deliberately missed her dates with Malcolm and went off to a dance-hall instead, especially in winter when there seemed little fun kissing and cuddling in the cabin of the boat. Yet sometimes, too, it seemed the cosiest thing out to sit there, with just the Welsh burner's globe giving its strawberry glow to their faces. Sheila brought her portable gramophone and anybody passing along the tow-path in the dead of December would have been surprised to hear *The Lambeth Walk* coming from a dark low barge in the snow.

On the evenings she stayed away from him, she knew what ache of disappointment he would be feeling. He stood like a horse alone in a field, head bent and patient. Even when she did come she would be late on purpose to watch his droopy accepting face light up. It suited her as yet that he did not think of anything further than kissing and cuddling, though she did begin to wonder whether he knew there was anything else.

Once, when she went off to the Majestic instead of keeping her date with him, he came after her. It took all his courage to enter the thumping hall and fetch her out.

'Good, there's going to be a bust-up over me,' she thought when she saw him barging his way across the floor. But

'O.K., O.K., she's all yours, dunna get your 'air off, mate,' her partner said, and Malcolm's set face looked silly with the relief.

Then when he got her outside, he hit her instead of the partner. She fell deliberately against the wall so that he should think he had hit her harder than he had. He was so stricken she almost had a fit of giggles. He bit his lip and twisted his hand and punched a lamp-post. She had got him now.

'Anna I good enough for thee?'

'It's not that at all.'

She almost said yes, but not in the way he meant. No *one* man was good enough. Each was all right up to a point, but not what she wanted all the time, exclusively. A man would need to have more sides to him than he, or perhaps any, could have. She trembled at her need, because her mother had said that a girl who could not be satisfied with one man was nothing but a prostitute. But Malcolm was not at all the kind of fellow Sheila had ever thought of marrying. It would be no life cooped up in a tumbledown cottage, not able to go about or have nice things because her man was a dim farmhand. Yet the barge and the canal-cottage seemed to exist in a fresher dimension. She would have laughed years back if someone had said this was what happiness would be like, but it was oddly how it was.

In the toughening of winter they resorted more and more to the hearth of the cottage. She had been shy there at first. Malcolm had persuaded her that the place needed a woman's touch, but when she went flipping round with a duster, Vincent said,

'Boatees anna gipsies, thee knowst.'

Then he sat looking at her, so that she was uncomfortable when Malcolm was out of the room. She fancied he was always making sure she and Malcolm did not creep off to bed together. Don't know why, she thought, I'm sure no harm'd come to his precious pal. It's me as'd suffer.

The snow gazed in at them seeming to watch their movements too. The silent world stretching into the distance made them move softly as if in a dream. Vincent would rise, ghostly, from his sleep and shuffle after them whenever they went into the kitchen or bedroom to be together. Why, Sheila asked herself, when we could easily have intercourse on the barge, supposing Malcolm knew there was such a thing? The youth seemed to have a sense of what was proper that oddly reminded her of Ernie. Every time he got to the threshhold of inter-course, the impetus went out of him and he sat back from the cuddle, dazed. She wanted to shake him and make him look straight at her instead of into some distant absence.

He knew very well what he should do at these points, but sex loomed so large as to render him helpless. Be-sides, he still resented the girl's intrusion into his life with Vincent and Bonzo, and he felt guilty at the change he had brought about for them. Winter had once been so easy, sitting by the fire reading his comics while Vincent carved ash-trays and pipes, and Bonzo lay exactly between their feet, eyes and ears cocking now and then from one side to the other, as if he felt the current that kept them in tune. Then old Simcox gave them a wireless that ran off a car-battery, and they discovered wonderingly new worlds.

'Well I never!' and 'Damn mey!' and 'Didst ever 'ear owt like it?' Vincent would exclaim as snatches of Euro-pean strife reached them subtly shaped by the B.B.C. voice.

Vincent had been always at hand. They still did their jobs together when he was well enough. At noon he had fetched their lunch to the fields, bread and cheese and water cress wrapped in a muslin cloth, and a jug of beer from the station pub. But a fall from a barn roof suddenly showed his frailty and winced up his blotting-paper features. His railway days were done. But he liked doing the cooking and cleaning at home and still took Malcolm his breakfasts and lunches. It frightened the youth to see the changes coming. Vincent had always seemed the same up to now, one who could not die, at least from inside. Yet here he was, helping to kill him off by bringing Sheila into their home. It was Vincent's image that always appeared to him, just when he had got worked up over her, hollowing him and drawing him back.

What was more, she alienated him terribly sometimes by saying.

'I don't want to worry you, Malc, but I reckon he's had it.'

When she said such things he wanted to biff her, mainly because they seemed more and more true.

On the other hand, he could not imagine life now without her coming of a Sunday and cooking the first dinners she had ever had to get. They were crude at first, raising a half-smile on Vincent's violet face. Gradually, though, even he grew to depend on her coming and washed himself scrupulously in preparation. There was a comfort in having a woman about even if she did want things different from the way they had been. And Sheila herself smiled wryly at the ease with which she had slipped into the way of being a man's woman, moving between the stove and table. It wasn't the streamlined kitchen she used to long for either: the water was pumped, the stove had to be stoked, its pots were heavy and black, and the sink was shallow fluted stone. She vowed never to do the men's washing, but one day that came naturally too and met no more objection than a smile in her. It was like playing house as a kid.

Every Sunday evening Vincent undid a large paisley neckerchief to count the silver threepenny bits he had saved in it. Sheila wondered, as she watched, whether he had ever had a love-affair before he was gassed.

XIII

'I expect you like to spend Christmas by the home-hearth.'

Mr. Cahill was more hesitant than usual and spoke from his shop-ladders, not looking at her. Liddy gave a part-nod and part-shrug.

'Perhaps you congregate at the Citadel?'

'Yes,' she replied, feeling unnaturally plural.

'You have a bit of fun.'

She did not know whether he was saying or asking, so she said,

'We go singing round the hospitals.'

'Would you be very disappointed to miss it for once?'

He kept shifting things on the shelves that were already straight.

'I hadn't thought.'

He craned his neck round.

'You see, it could be the last proper Christmas for some time now.'

She became terribly conscious of his feet hidden in their tight triangular shoes.

'Oh, don't say things like that.'

He came down the steps quickly, a tin of Fynnon Salts in his hand. He looked gravely into her eyes and she looked gravely down at his shoes.

'They'll be too strong for us this time. They've got Science on their side.'

She backed away, feeling herself already up against

'their' strength. He held the tin of salts as if it contained Science. The shop's clock ticked loudly into the looming spaces.

'So would you like to come here—to me—for Christmas?'

She nodded and

'I was hoping you'd ask,' her dry throat managed to say, though she hadn't hoped till now.

'Ah,' he breathed, and put the tin back on the shelf.

It snowed. When Liddy had stepped over the silent oblongs of the streets, Ernie said to his grandma,

'I didn't think she'd go when it came to the push.'

'Oh, 'er knows what 'er's doing all right. 'er's got 'er 'ead screwed on.'

That seemed to be true of all girls, if Mrs. Hordell was to be trusted, and hardly ever of lads. Ernie peeped through the blackout into the flaky dark and saw Liddy's head in its white tam and thought how well screwed on it looked. She walked so surely that for the first time in his life he felt a pang at seeing her go. He had regarded her as a fixture in life along with everything else and now, like everything else, she was becoming the usual phantom. Grandad had gone, and the cat. One of his favourite budgerigars had a growth. Seeing the procession of losses and wondering how it came to be called life, he raced to the door.

'Whatever's up?' he heard his grandma cry, ever-ready to panic.

'Nothing. Sit you still.'

He opened the front door but the swoosh of cold air and his awareness of only having slippers on his feet stopped him from dashing out to the solitary figure now turning the corner and asking it to come back.

'Put that light out,' came a laughing voice from across the street. He turned back indoors to his grandma's fire and sat thinking of Liddy's heartbreaking ordinariness, how dependable she was and, in a world of loss, how necessary. Could the feeling be love? It seemed not to be—it was too flat.

'I wonder if she loves him,' he murmured.

His grandma flashed her glasses round on him through the firelight.

'Dunna be so daft. A man that age?'

'Well, it couldn't be money our Liddy'd go after.'

'Lad, you dunna know what girls goo after. She's 'ad nowt all her life, poor soul. She deserves a bit of luxury. Push that chestnut with the poker, not with yer foot. I wouldna stand in 'er way. You'll burn them new slippers.'

Liddy had bought the slippers for him. Examining them anxiously, shall I stand in her way, he asked himself. There wouldn't be much point. She would probably walk straight over him as everybody else did. Nobody could be expected to stop for what he had to offer. Besides—how everybody kept on saying it—there was a war on.

Liddy felt she was going on a long journey through a dream-landscape, the streets were that empty. It seemed like the last Christmas ever and there was nobody left to celebrate it except herself. She almost would have liked it that way, but throttled the wicked idea with a twist of her chin into her white scarf. Everything altered at a shift of feeling. Life had been tense with significance once; now it was nothing. What did it matter that her nose was reddening and her eyes running? Did she need to look beautiful—well, nice, since beauty had never been in the question—for Mr. Cahill? Did she, to put it another way, love him? He would ask her today. Harold, Harold. She had to get used to using the name. He checked her when 'Mr. Cahill' came so readily, so deferentially to her lips. If it was love, love was a very peculiar thing. Would he have a turkey for her? Would he be at the stove in an apron, smelling of onions? Harold. If it was a dream, he wasn't the dream-man.

Nor was he in an apron. The cooking had been done and he wore new flannels and cardigan over a white shirt. Her heart turned when she saw that his plaid tie was the one she had given him. She let him kiss her, just a quick bob. If only she knew whether he was more than a piece of animated flesh in front of her, distinguished from others only by happening to be there. How could she possibly know if she loved him?

'Come by the fire. Sit you down, take your shoes off and open this.'

He handed her a neat parcel and knelt with heavy breaths, watching while her careful fingers undid the string, rolled it up, put back the paper, folded it and at last opened the box inside. She knew what was going to be there. He rubbed her feet and covered them with the fussy twinkling slippers which, after she had smelt and caressed them, she handed to him, first one, then the other. Her toes curled like cats, as if they at least were in love with him, as he tenderly placed her feet on the fender. The sequins flashed warmly between its warm brass knobs.

'Now what about a cuppa? With whisky.'

'Ooh, only a drop.'

'Get away with you—only a drop! It's Christmas Day, and this isn't the workhouse, either.'

Why did he say that? His jokes were never very good. She looked at him unsmiling, and he looked at her and felt himself losing his zest. He dashed to the kitchen so that he would not have to face their separateness. He had made a picture of her, soft, obedient, thoughtful, but her looks at him came close to smashing it.

She sat back and took in the decorations. Fancy, he had gone to all this trouble, just for her: streamers, holly, crackers on the side-plates, Santas on the cake. The furniture gleamed in the firelight; and cards stood everywhere, making him seem a most important and well-known man.

'Did Mrs. Cahill like Christmas? I mean, did she like decorating and that?'

'Yes, but these are special. There'll be—sugar?—no more this side of an armistice. And that means there'll be no more full stop.'

Liddy shivered and sipped her tea thankfully.

'Ooh, it's nice.'

She wished she didn't always talk about Mrs. Cahill. It was as if they had nothing else in common. Perhaps it was the house that did it, the offended spirit hovering in its shadows, particularly in its empty wardrobe.

'It's grand spending Christmas with somebody else again. I was all on my own last year, you know. Elsie'd not long gone then. My sister in Chester wanted me to go over there, but I couldn't bring myself to just then. I could've gone this time, but there was no need, thanks to you.'

'However did you go on, cooped up all on your own?'

Her heart warmed to him. 'I should've got suicidal, I think.'

'I did a bit.'

'And all those bottles of stuff down in the shop.' She shuddered for him.

'Are you glad I didn't, Liddy?'

'Of course I am.'

'No, really glad—for yourself, I mean.'

She smiled nervously.

'Mmm.' She resorted to her tea.

'There was no fear of it really.' He got up to take her cup and saucer. 'I don't hold with those antics. Suicide's against nature. It's the coward's way.'

'Yes.' Liddy nodded woodenly.

'Perhaps not in every case,' he hastily added, reddening as he recollected Liddy's mother. 'Sometimes the mind is that—er—upset, it doesn't know what it's doing.'

'Yes.'

'But—for me it would have been cowardly.'

'Yes.'

'I'll just go and get the eats.'

'I'll come and help.'

'Sit you down. I shan't always wait on you, you know.' He tried to wink, but nerves made it a wince.

'But I don't like sitting here by meself. I'd rather come and talk to you.'

Once she saw his pathos she felt easier. Perhaps she could love him or at least something of that sort. She was not afraid any more. He tied an apron round her, softly shaping her waist between his hands.

She gaped when she saw the spread. It was like the last fling before a long fast.

'I hope you didn't have much dinner.'

'Just a bit of pork.'

It had actually been one of Mrs. Hordell's whopping meals.

'Never know what you'll get with 'im,' the old lady had laughed. 'Might be nowt but a coupla pills.'

The pair worked well together, did not get in each other's way and, except for exaggerated politeness, wasted no time. She did the bread and trimmings and he sliced the bird. Gradually she took over and he watched with joy her quiet coping ways. He escorted her ceremoniously back to the sitting-room, where he gave her sherry to drink while he fetched things in and changed his cardigan for a smart waistcoat. She looked at the firelight through her glass and didn't care about the world.

They pulled their crackers and he poured dark red wine. They drank, ate, chatted and laughed till she swam in hot gold. She had felt such unfocussing flopsiness only once before, and she knew it was all she wanted.

'D'you know what I'd like to do now?' she giggled.

'What?'

'Have a go on your pianola.'

The pianola had been shut since Mrs. Cahill's death. He rose in unsteady grandeur and opened the lid of the stool and held up each roll at arm's length.

'What'll it be, Madame? *Rustle of Spring, Roses are Blooming in Picardy*, or Handel's—pardon—*Largo*?

'None of them. Something quick.'

'*Take a Pair of Sparkling Eyes*—will that do?'

He sparkled his eyes into hers.

'Okey-dokey.' She twirled towards him and, as he caught her and placed her on the stool, she gave a loud belch.

'Ooh, 'ark at me.'

'Should you require an aid to digestion, you have only to say the word and I'll pop downstairs.'

'Pop *is* the word.'

They guffawed, swaying together. He fixed the dusty roll. At first she could not get the knack for laughing and the music sprinkled out in irrelevant bursts. Then she got it and pedalled away happily absorbed in the sound, really feeling that she was making it. She thought of the joy Ernie must have got from playing. She tried several rolls and, getting used to the rhythm, started thumping furiously at her feet, laughing till the tears streamed down her face and she fell straight back from the stool into Mr. Cahill's ready arms.

'That's enough now.'

He carried her to the fireside chair, her head in a fuddle. While she rested he held her hand. She lay, aware of his discretion. He took no advantage. She began to wish he would, and became aware of herself playing with his hand and drawing it to her. Fears jabbed through her fuzziness and she woke as out of a trance. He was gazing at her.

'I haven't given you your other present yet. I was afraid you might not want it.'

She sat up.

'What is it?'

'Are you in a fit state to come and see?'

He led her to the icy bedroom and she was wide awake. She did not flinch, knowing she could trust him if not herself. On the dressing-table was a small imitation Christmas tree with frosty decorations.

'Look.'

She looked, a puzzled smile on her face. She did not see it, and he was put out.

'There, there.'

It was a ring, of course, at the tip of the tree, a solitaire diamond.

'Oh how lovely.'

She had put it on before she realised.

'You don't mind then?' he asked softly.

She did something she had not done for ages: she burst into tears.

'What is it?'

She shook her head, not knowing herself.

'Do you like it?'

She nodded, sobbing still, and put her arms round him. He drew her on to the bed.

'Now I don't want you to say yes till I've told you something. Give it to me.'

She took the ring off, handed it to him, and waited. She watched his hands clench and unclench. She suppressed a series of stuffing belches, hoping he would not choose this moment to kiss her. But she noticed his hairy nostrils stretch, and once or twice, as he spoke, his voice wavered over similar suppressions. She studied the pull of his trousers over his thighs and the veins like streaks of dirt in the back of his hands.

'We spoke once—remember?—I asked you—just before your brother died——'

He smoothed the green quilt.

'Yes?'

'About—you know—such children being born.'

'Yes. You said they shouldn't be.'

He shifted uneasily.

'And you agreed with me, didn't you?'

'Yes.'

'Ah.' His breathing was like time, trying to measure the

meaning of the silence. 'If we get—if we got—married, would you want to have children?' She knew it. She did not move a muscle. His hand was dead on the satin cover.

'I don't know. Not if you didn't, p'raps. I wouldn't mind if you didn't want.'

He sighed.

'But,' she couldn't help going on, 'they needn't be like Clive, need they?'

'You could never be sure.'

'Don't you *want* children?' She turned fully at him. 'Don't you even want to *try*?'

'Suppose I can't. I'm not saying I can't, mind you, but just suppose?'

She glanced, against herself, at his trouser-flies. The image of her brother's curled privates came into her mind. She imagined a space between Mr. Cahill's legs, a bald web of skin. He watched her eyes and held his legs closer together. She did not speak.

'Would you mind that much?'

She still did not speak.

'I thought you wouldn't want to—I mean, seeing how you were placed, with your brother——'

'I don't know. I shall have to think. I'd better be going now.'

She suddenly noticed how cold she was, sweating and cold.

'Oh, it's not time yet. You can stay. You don't have to say yes just so as to stay. I understand. Only stay, won't you?'

'I'll have to think—on me own somewhere.'

She went to the door and he followed as if she were an important customer. He hurried for her coat. She noticed patches of sweat above his waistcoat arm-holes.

'Oh,' she said, entering the sitting-room, 'there's all this washing-up.'

'Never mind, it'll be all right.'

He seemed now to be dying to get rid of her, as if he endorsed her view of him. But as he opened the front door for her and she stepped out,

'Heavens!' she cried out, 'I've still got me slippers on.'

He dashed for her shoes. She handed the damp slippers to him and, scarcely into the warm shoes, turned away into the brisk air. She searched the hardening film of snow with her little torch, moving determinedly home. Home. Even before she got there, she knew she could not go in. She stood outside the window gazing at a chink in the blackout, left by Ernie when he had looked out for her. She heard him tinkling carols on the piano. She did not know that he was wishing she would come back. Mrs. Hordell and Mrs. Fetchford were drinking steadily in the firelight. Liddy could not bring herself to face them. It was a home but not her home. She ached for one of her own that she might order as she pleased. A vision of Mr. Cahill's neat shelves of jars and tubes made her cavernous with longing. She moved directionless, round and round the park railings for an hour nearly.

A glow drew her to where people shuffled and stamped about the pavement. She would not normally have entered a Catholic church, but its waxy warmth lured her in. She wished she had gone singing with the Army after all, busied with the feeling of the day rather than her own feelings. In every corner candles changed the space into hot light and for a while it seemed there was no substance in the world at all. Liddy sat hypnotised, though fearful of being turned out. Eventually the flames began to be dowsed by shadowy figures. The last lights to go were in front of the Virgin, where a woman in fusty fox-furs knelt, muttering through bass-voiced sobs. Along one of the pews a tramp with wild popping eyes and hair like Jack Frost's, the smell of his tweed-rag coat piercing wax and incense, counted out coins with rheumaticky fingers. A young priest tiptoed up to him, nervously affable, but the tramp hunched sharply away as if he intended to eat his money. The priest passed on to the lady in furs, re-setting his smile and gently touching her shoulder. She let out a faint screech and bent round with a twisty grin. Liddy sank into the shadows before the priest came on to her. She was thinking of Mr. Cahill at his sinkful of dishes. Lonely. Lonely. She forced her heart into pity of him, but it was her own loneliness that really moved her. The tramp and the woman in furs had nowhere particular to go, and they showed her her own life as what it was.

When she tiptoed from the church, hearing keys clinking in its shades, there was no doubt where she was going. Yet when she reached the pharmacist's doorway, she could not ring the bell. She looked up to see if any lights were still on, but his blinds were predictably thorough. She wandered away again, then stopped at the corner, furious with herself. I shall. I shall. She stooped to a ginger cat that arked its backbone at her leg. I shall. Beggars can't be choosers. Besides, *he's* the beggar.

He seemed more amazed than thrilled to find her on the doorstep, as if he had settled himself already to doing without her. Perhaps he even resented her return, although tears rose to his pale dug-down eyes.

'I thought I'd come back.'

'Ah.'

'If you'd really like me to, that is.'

He smiled. He had to like her to now.

She entered and he took her coat.

'I'd rather be called Liddy than Ginger,' she said.

'That's all right then, don't worry now. Just put your slippers on.'

He knelt in front of her and put them softly on her feet. She looked round.

'Have you done the washing up?'

XIV

The spring was really no more beautiful than usual, but Sheila had never felt it to the full before or been so involved in it. She saw it happen not only in old Simcox's fields, but also on her way to work. Being so much out of doors, her skin took on the glow it used and was meant to have. Malcolm bronzed too and looked really handsome, as if the gold worked somehow from the inside. Sometimes when they walked she felt herself suspended above their bodies and, in the span of shades and light, saw the rightness of their being together. Other times, though, she wondered. It seemed she had to make all the moves. He still hadn't got beyond kissing. When they came into the cottage for Sunday tea, Vincent would ask,

'Wheer'st bin?'

And they would reply,

'Just a walk.'

'Wowk, wowk, wowk, dost do nowt but wowk?'

No, Sheila would feel like saying, nowt, nix, not a damn thing.

On fine Sundays they boated along the cut the way her sharp memory recognised so readily. She took Malcolm to see 'Judder's Gulch' where the barge-boy had frightened her years before. She half wished Malcolm would frighten her a bit, but he didn't. Tufts of primroses lit the damp dark bottoms of the cliffs, and Sheila snuffled them, standing away in frustration at the impossibility of holding on to their scent.

'Thee'dst smell 'em a lot berrer if thee didsna smeowk.'

She shook her head.

'It's not that.'

He could see she was in tears and he didn't know what to do.

She couldn't think why she cried, but she supposed it was to do with the way the flowers came and went so quickly and there was no knowing about them. It was to do with the war as well.

He stood like his dog, staring at her, wishing he could see inside her head and read her thoughts.

On the first summery day he took her to a woodland patch which seemed to be spotlit by the sun and sheltered by yellow-green walls of heat.

'I used to run rind 'ere like a redskin,' he said.

'Naked?'

'Near enough.' He blushed.

'It's certainly very private,' she mused, thinking everywhere they went was very private, yet for all the use they made of it they might as well have been watched by a million pairs of prudish eyes.

Let's just see what he does, she thought, and she took off her blouse. Then, fixing him with a humourous slant, she flirted her bra undone.

'Stoppit!' He got up and tried not to look.

'Well, you did, didn't you? I want to get tanned everywhere, not just in patches like an old cow.'

She looked down distastefully at her breasts starkly white against her brown neck and belly. She was proud of their shape, though, and felt they weren't seen often enough even by herself. When she patted them, he jerked his head away.

'Don't be soft, lad. Who's to see us? Come on, you as well.'

She knelt up to tug at his buttons.

'Geroff, geroff!' He snatched fiercely away and scampered into the trees.

'Malk. Malk.'

But he did not answer. She shrugged and slipped off her skirt and pantees and lay back, smiling just slightly. His tread in the woodgrowth made her wonder what it was kept them together when they were of such different worlds and had such different ways. Nobody could say it was sex. Just habit, she supposed.

He stopped suddenly. Bluebells flooded the ground, they took over the whole wood, useless and all there for the taking. He trod reverently forward and then crouched over the purple curlicue heads, holding on to a beech sapling for balance and gazing at the girl where she lay, irrelevant, like the flowers among the fresh grass. He could not decide whether he wanted to run on her or to go further and further off. He began picking the flowers, slobbering slightly like something possessed, till he had a huge sheaf. He rushed out of the wood with them and stood above the girl, who did not move. But when he saw her pubic hair, he stepped back and threw the bluebells on her to hide it. She was watching from the corner of her eye. The flowers made her jump, but she forced herself to stay lying down, stretched out. She hoped there were no spiders in them. This is it, she thought, relaxing and tensing by turns. But it wasn't. His footsteps crashed away from her, back into the trees, and instead of him she pressed the bluebells to her. They squeaked and bruised gummily between her arms and legs, and their scent flared up into her taut face. She was going to call him to her, but

'No,' she said to herself bitterly, 'I shan't.'

When she looked up, he was sitting astride a tree-trunk tormenting ants with a twig.

'Big soft kid,' she muttered.

She turned over, shook the bluebells off her irritably and let them die in the sun.

The pair did not speak again till she put her clothes back on. Even then he could only say,

'Shall's goo back wom now?'

She did not answer but walked the path to the boat, in silence behind him. He tried to take her hand now and then, but she snatched it away.

When they reached the cottage he dashed indoors, alarmed at not having heard Bonzo's usual bark. Vincent was lying flat on the kitchen floor, the brown tea-pot smashed across the flags as if he had spat it out of his purple face along with some other substance, blood and slime, that still gurgled in his windpipe. Malcolm gathered the deadweight of cloth and flabby flesh to him, while Sheila turned against the window, her hands to her mouth, whispering loudly,

'It's judgement on us.'

She did not know why she said it. It was the sort of thing her mother would say and she herself would normally scorn. She could have kicked herself for say-ing it now, because Malcolm was staring at her with a fixed hating look that made her realise she had voiced his unformed thought and made it true for him.

'Leave me on me own with 'im.'

She flushed with rage at being rendered meaningless. She hovered a moment, then decided to make the tea straight into the cups. There was some safety and significance in juggling with them. But Malcolm went on crouching with Vincent in his arms. And when she laid a cup beside him, saying,

'Try giving him a sip. Haven't you got brandy or something? Now we'll *have* to get a doctor,' all he said was

'Leave us alone.'

So she did. Setting her lips, she straightened herself and went. He would realise his need of her when she had gone. He would come running. Along the towpath she slowed her steps and glanced back, in half a mind to return and *make* him want her with him. Ahead of her, over Hanley, a bouquet of barrage-balloons dreamed comfortably in the sky. What would he do? Lie there and die with Vincent? Bury the corpse in the garden without letting anybody know? Then perhaps live as a hermit, getting maggotty and queer. Maybe he would sink the body in the cut and then do himself in. But she didn't care. He had told her to go. Let him go and get called up. She would never see him again. He was a washout as a lover any way. Bugger him.

XV

She had just got used to doing without him when he turned up again. It was a damp summer Sunday. He could not for shyness knock at the door but waited at the street-end, hoping she would come out to its gloamy greyness. She had hated Sundays since their parting. Lads were being called up like summoned souls, to disappear as fast and mysteriously as the armaments she made. Soon there would be nobody but a collier or two to go out with. There was little to do but traipse round the vacant sad-eyed, sand-bagged town and watch the evacuees come labelled from London and the shop-windows being criss-crossed with tape. Mr. Cahill's were so neatly done they seemed to show the satisfaction Liddy got from helping him. Liddy's not daft, Sheila said to herself, an old man's the best bet now. Mr. Cahill was an A.R.P. warden and occasionally Sheila would see him and Liddy, silly in helmets and groundsheets, rushing out of the depot for a practice invasion. The Jerries might have been at the suburbs so grim and urgent-faced the wardens were, unravelling their hose-pipes, tapping the mucky hydrants, pumping their stirrups and wetting the streets with their futile jets.

'Fat lot of good they'll be when the Nazis do come,' Sheila muttered, though she didn't really think they would come anyway. Her dad had refused to bother with a shelter or a gas-mask and never left his bed when the sirens cried in the night.

But Sheila enjoyed dashing next door with her mother, to sleep on a communal straw mattress, exchanging tense whispers about 'ours' and 'theirs', in the earthy ear-wiggy darkness.

She tried not to look too glad when she found Malcolm, hands in pockets, leaning against a lamp-post outside her home.

'Well, if it isn't George Formby.' She strummed an imaginary ukelele at him.

But his first words went through her.

'I've gone and got meself co'ed up.' He laughed to cover things he could not say.

She never thought of it happening to him. He seemed to be outside the ordinary population whose names appeared on registers. But

'I thought as much,' she replied drily, not to show her feelings. 'Army'll just suit you.'

Then, after they had walked alongside each other a while, they kissed in an entry.

He did not tell her that he had come more because he missed Vincent than because he missed her. After the burial he had boarded the cottage up and gone to live with old Simcox on his farm. He still couldn't understand why his pattern of life had had to stop. He cursed the day it did. Old Simcox and his dog had been Vincent's only mourners beside himself. The home-made coffin was brought out and roped to a hand-cart. Malcolm and Simcox pushed it to Eric's van waiting at the lane-end. The rutted ground was filled with puddles that stared whitely up as the cart-wheels trundled over them. Bonzo's eyes also had this blankness, in contrast to the collie's black sparkles that seemed to know what was being lost. Then Tyke, as Simcox typically called

148

him, sniffed at Bonzo's bottom and they thrilled each other in a glistening tremor. Malcolm suddenly wondered why anybody cared about anything at all. Simcox dowsed his chewed-looking cigarette by way of last respects. When the van moved off, the bull-terrier dashed to shout like a maniac at its wheels till old Simcox flicked his fingers and it stopped, seemingly in mid-bark.

Malcolm had always admired that snap of the fingers and wished he could use it to whisk Sheila back to him again. But it wasn't till his call-up papers came that he decided to go and see her. At first he thought it would be a good excuse to take the papers along to her so that she could help him fill them in, but then he knew she would laugh at him, so he did them with Simcox breathing smokily down his neck.

It seemed the most natural thing in the world to Sheila to resume her Sundays with Malcolm and, because the time was so short, they met evenings and Saturdays as well. She did not know whether she had loved him before and she did not know whether she loved him now, but it seemed that if she did *not* love him now, she would never love anybody. As for him, he wasn't sure at first whether she meant any more to him than possibilities he had in view but when he re-opened his cottage with her, he knew she did. She meant what the fields meant, in fact, and his dead friend, and his dog. She was home. She looked after him. It was like a honeymoon, but neither mentioned marriage. Sheila felt it would be bad luck to bring it up. If she showed the need to hang on to him, she would surely lose him. But she often lay over him, clambering him down and crying,

'Don't go. Bugger them. Don't go.'

'Dunna mind so much,' he whispered, embarrassed and frightened by her fear and the force of her flesh, wanting to go just to get away from her.

She would sit up from him, studying his body and thinking of it falling apart before her eyes. She grasped at him, wishing there was more time just to know what she felt. Sometimes she pushed him off and they spent a whole day in gloomy silence, glancing like hostile children at each other, locked away in their own hot selves.

Once he went off with old Simcox and she heard shots from the woods. Men are so silly, she thought, the way they get their satisfactions. She left off washing his socks and ran out across the fields, getting her legs buttercup-dusted. For no particular reason she wanted to put herself in the way of one of the bullets. Just to spoil their fun. It would serve him right. But she wasn't sure who she meant by 'him'.

She climbed the stone wall into the glade, where the air seemed to be smoke-blue strings on which a million insects zithered. Apart from them there was no sound, as if all the animals were waiting, holding their breath, to see who would be next for death.

Then she saw the men stalking through the trees far off. She bobbed down. I'll show them, she thought, not knowing how she could or why she wanted to. A shot seemed to divide the winged air and set its filminess all in a zigzag. Something slithered to the ground not far from her. She dashed towards it. It was a wood-pigeon. Its white neck was scorched, but its breast still breathed and its eyes glared ever open, watching everything. It saw, before she did, Bonzo come charging to snatch it just as Sheila had softly raised it warm and full in her hands. A wing tore between them and she screamed. She hit and kicked the dog in a fury till Malcolm came and drew Bonzo in his arms and loved him, looking up at her with disgust. Old Simcox, chuckling behind them, took the broken bird and twisted its neck. Sheila turned on him, flashing her eyes up and down from his leather-bound calves to the thick white hair that sprung straight above his eyebrows.

'Grown men! Grown men!' Then it was Malcolm's turn. 'War's about all you're fit for. Well, go and get killed in it and good riddance!'

She ran off, telling herself she was sick of him, weary with her own emotions. She would never come again. The picture of Simcox's calves creaking together in their gaiters kept coming into her mind.

But she went back, the day before Malcolm joined up. They hardly dared to speak. Bonzo merely growled. But, filled with gradual pity for each other, the lovers went to their familiar places. Malcolm carved their names in the stone of a bridge. And that was that. They had brief intervals together during his training, then the longer stretch of embarkation leave, and then he went to Africa in the 8th Army. It was clear that he was glad to be going, because it would be simpler than staying. It was simpler for her, too, and she had to cry very hard to stop herself feeling a certain relief.

XVI

The vacant cottage began to decay. Doors and windows sprang open in the wind: leaves flushed the cobwebby corners; spiders and earwigs extended their businesses which then got lost under snow. One March night a gale dragged the corrugated bits of the roof off. Primroses and celandines grew as usual, while Malcolm, not having seen the world's wonders that Vincent had promised him, was blown to bits at Tobruk. So Sheila put it later when the news had sunk in. Reading his letters before she knew he was dead, she had almost wanted to be rid of him. They seemed so ignorant, so bloody stupid. Bad enough hearing him talk like that, but to see it written down! No, the words misrepresented him. He could put so little of himself in them, only the dumb-bell side. And now he was nothing, not even a dumb-bell. If things wanted it like that, she would not let herself be tormented by them. All over the world people were hearing such news and sitting blarting their eyes out and getting nowhere. It made her blood boil. The stupidity of suffering! Just letting it come, letting it do what it liked and not smashing back. She punched her fist into the air. Damn it. Bloody bloody bloody. Shit to the thing that Ernie Hordell oh so typically believed in. If Ernie had been there at that moment she would have throttled him on the spot.

Her inside seemed turned outside, nerves exposed to people's voices and movements and their attempts to find out what was the matter with her. She felt clanged between sheets of grey metal. She could not cry. Perhaps she would throw herself into the cut, but that would be just what He or It or Whatever-it-was wanted. Instead she walked like a zombie to the cottage. But she could not bring herself to go in at its dead door. She climbed on to a bridge and gazed over the fields that flared and puffed with blossom. Her eye caught blue gaps at the wood's edge. She ran across the wide space, dodging thistles and cow-pats, and stopped only when she reached the bluebells. She stared at them, her senses somersaulting. They waited, hushed, aware. And then, pressed by a grey weight of clouds, they breathed at her as one being their creamy breath that rooted her with them. Some were broken and there was a flattened white-stalked trail through them. The air seemed conscious of itself, darkly concentrated.

'Do you know I'm here?'

She heard her own voice as if it were somebody else's. She did not know whether she was speaking to the flowers or to the lad whose name she could not bring herself to say. She trod forward, stooping now and then to pick up the broken flowers till she had a juicy handful. She pressed them in her blouse as if she got something from them.

'Wherever are you? What did you go and——?'

Talking to me bloody self now.

But the notion that Malcolm had made his way through the purple earth-cloud ahead of her persisted.

I must be going crackers or something.

She smiled as a bee tried to squeeze inside one of the bells of her bouquet. She watched it work near her hand and even felt its legs rest fleetingly on her skin.

Then she saw Bonzo. He belonged to the farm now, but every day he sniffed round his old home to see if Malcolm and Vincent were back.

'Bonzo,' she called. 'Come on, here, come on.'

But he looked indifferently at her and then barked his loud automatic toneless bark.

'Oh, bugger you then.'

She had always detested him any way.

They backed away from each other. The rock-like cloud burst open and soaked them both to the skin.

XVII

Ernie was at the NAAFI piano, drawing a stringy sing-song from the airmen and airwomen. A Polish accordionist jogged round him, grinning with brown and gold teeth, not seeming to mind that he did not understand the chatter. When his fingers tingled to move into a folk-song and bring a memory of home, the moronic voices dragged him back to *The Anniversary Waltz*. Ernie wondered whether the Pole was screaming inside with the pain of being alien, but there was no telling under that grateful-gormless grin.

Trousered and turbanned waitresses battled round the clamorous tables. The tea they dealt was putrid, coating the gaping mouths. Two disabled soldiers of the First War collected cups, jigging up and down on crippled legs. Notices made the walls lurid, one saying they had ears, one warning against the Squander Bug, another proclaiming *Jesus lives!*, a fourth telling people where to go with syphilis. The red religious word caught Ernie's eye as he sipped his tea between tunes. It was Easter Sunday. It ought to be true, he mused, and began to play *Jesus Lives! Thy terrors now*. The terrors came from where the hymn came from, where Bach and Schumann and nearly all Ernie's best-beloved music came from.

Hands plonked on his shoulders and tea-breathed voices shouted against the 'fucking hymn', so he modulated into *Lilli Marlene*. It pleased him to think

155

that both hymn and song would be being sung some-where across the Rhine, on a camp just like this one. *Their* terrors came from here. Me, a terror—what a laugh, he thought.

At the end of the song he turned to his tomato roll, but he could not eat for the lump in his throat. The peppery tomato smell reminded him of home, and of his grandma now in hospital. Anything was possible now. If only he had been there when the siren cried and she had rushed to the cellar as if there were a million bombs already in the air. She and Mrs. Fetchford sat waiting over their ale every night, the one tense, the other exultant. There were no raids, but when the siren sounded Mrs. Hordell rushed round like a flabby demon, shouting,

''anley's down. It's flat.'

Mrs. Fetchford followed her, chuckling, into the drain-scented cellar. But that night the dog got in the way, and Mrs. Hordell fell thud. Her thick glasses smashed across the grid, while in the other woman's torchlight a spider scuttled out of the way as if taking part of the spilt consciousness with it. For, when she came to in hospital, Grandma was not herself any more. She ought to have died, everybody said when they saw her, parti-cularly Mr. Cahill. Then she would not have embar-rassed them with childishness.

Ernie's compassionate leaves were the worst experi-ences of his life. He sat in the darkness of his old home, alone. One of his first jobs was to get the dog destroyed. Now he had got to decide about the other belongings. He wished he could destroy them too, along with him-self. Liddy had invited him to stay with her and Mr. Cahill, but he could not face their dutiful sympathy.

156

Besides, Mr. Cahill had refused to take the dog, even though Liddy had wanted it, because, he said, animals spread germs.

His grandma's state beggared the faith she had fostered in him. She was being systematically blotted out, all the care and feeling she had stood for and put into his life drained off. There in place of Grandma was an ancient rubbery baby eating and messing her bed.

'The dim bitch went and twisted up and closed her big fat thighs and nearly castrated me.'

Back in the NAAFI's din a bright spark of a corporal was holding a group of lads pop-eyed as usual. The Pole played him a sentimental accompaniment. The pop eyes cocked up at a waitress over the edges of cups. She affected a heard-it-all-before indifference but stayed around to empty saucers and fag-ends and wipe tables with her filthy cloth.

'I had to slap her unconscious, then prise her pins open. Ripped half me fucking foreskin off in the process.'

'Bloody liar,' lilted a Welsh voice.

'Let's have a look,' a Londoner chimed in.

'I swear to you—anybody got a Bible?' He looked slily at Ernie. 'No, I thought not. Well, I have. I keep it for my daily devotions—comes in useful when you find there's no paper in the bog.'

Amid brays the corporal produced a soft-covered Gospel from the pocket over his heart.

'Here's one for you, Ernie. How can you tell when you're really in love with a bint?'

Ernie drew back. It seemed as if he had asked the question himself. The men guffawed and muttered silly answers.

'Shall I tell him?'

157

'Yes!' The chorus came from wet, breathy, fleshy faces, nothing but faces,

'When you can clean your teeth with her shit.'

Ernie got up and left his cream-bun behind him. Looking back he saw a swirl of sweaty heads and unco-ordinated limbs. He hovered outside round the latrines, unsure whether he wanted to go in or what he wanted to do.

He wandered over the twilight camp and everything he saw told him that sex was all there was between men and women. There was no time for anything else but war and sex. And it was just like God's love, destroying the old, raging after novelty: the past, shared memories, neighbourliness and affection were of no account against it. Sheila came into his mind as the stranger she was, someone other than the girl he used to play with.

Couples smooched in doorways and against walls, wherever there was darkness and no police patrolling. Some were police anyway. It was a shadow-act of mass defiance against lurking death. What had he ever known, Ernie wondered, of the grown-up Sheila—or even Liddy? He had a brief vision of his steely fingers caressing their breasts as if they were straddling chords. He shivered at the thought of all the never-to-be known mystery of women.

Stars came crisp over hut and hangar against the green west. He took deep breaths, his stuffy nose clearing with the scour of North Sea air. At the edge of the camp a Lancaster, ripped and gutted, stood in sad silhouette. Through the wire fence Ernie looked eastward to where the night steeped over Europe. A queer medley of sounds wafted out from the nearby billets. A light flared in one and was quickly put out at a protest. Twined with

Forces' Favourites came from some unlikely station a Bach chorale, for whose German words Ernie knew the English version:

> *He gives the winds their courses*
> *And bounds the ocean's shore.*

The trees seemed to hear it, feather-leaves pricked up against the light part of the sky. Behind, the huts crouched in shadow. *Easter Sunday*, Ernie said to himself over and over, forcing it to be meaningful to him. Something moved in the field. Sheep. They had been still as stones till then. When the ewe moved, two lambs knelt up bleating and dashed to her, butting each other out of the way. Ernie felt that when the war ended it might be possible to set about making a world like *Nowhere*, where every alive soul would move in a pattern like Bach's, but then an owl screeched and a WAAF laughed from the gym wall and he found he had pins and needles in one leg. And, at that moment, bombers setting off on night-missions rammed up the sky like dragons and drilled the world to its marrow.

XVIII

'I wondered when you were going to realise it was me. I dare say's it was me hair that put you off.'

Sheila had gone blonde, and Ernie *was* put off by the dead-ended frizz but said,

'It's very nice—just like Betty Hutton.'

'Harpo Marx, you mean. Come to see your gra'ma?'

He nodded. They were on the hospital steps. The city lay exposed below them, gas-holders, bottle-ovens, spires and slag-heaps crimsoned by the evening sun, tender as the innards of a body on an operating table.

'Is she any better?'

He shook his head, still taut with what he had seen: her eyes hollowing, skin between her old breasts blotched as with mud. She was always trying to twine her hair back into its ear-phones. Then her fingers jerked and fumbled round the Fry's Cream Bar he had brought her. Her mouth was like a perished rubber washer.

'She'll never be better till she's dead.'

Still the same morbid bugger, Sheila said to herself. But somehow she was glad he was what he was. And now that she looked at him, he seemed quite presentable, broader, healthy-coloured at last. His catarrh had gone even.

'What're *you* doing here, Sheila? Hope nobody's poorly.'

'Only me.'

He looked a question with his face, but behind it he

was still hearing his grandma saying, 'Dunna go, lad, dunna leave me,' while 'Ta-ta' he called, desperately jolly, in reminder of her beloved Tommy Handley. She did not say her usual 'for now' but simply looked into the air where he had been.

Sheila was patting her belly.

'Don't tell me you haven't noticed.'

It wasn't really as big as she imagined and most men would not have noticed.

He looked very dubious, entertaining suspicions. She laughed sharply. She had never seen the point of keeping secrets and preferred being known as pregnant to being thought fat.

'That's it, duck. I'm in the club.'

He did not know what to say, hating the way she put it but guessing her strange embarrassment. Too hurriedly she filled a pause, having got used to doing so.

'Well, it's only what you might expect, isn't it? I don't think anybody's been surprised.'

It got her goat to catch her work-mates' nods and side-looks and to hear the chief clerk say. 'Miss Rownall —it is still Miss, isn't it?' when she had gone to sign off.

'Are you going to get married then?'

That would be Ernie's first consideration of course.

'Who to?'

His glasses reflected pink sunshine on a concrete wall. Poppies like tissue were splitting their capsules, and hot brown-scented wallflowers seemed to launch bees born of their own petals into the air.

'I always fancied meself as a G.I. bride. But he's 'opped it. Liberating Italy or something.'

'He'll come back though?'

'He's showing no signs. I haven't had a word from him. He may be dead for all I know. They all die on me. I wish to God I'd joined up like I once thought I would.'

'It could happen anywhere.' Ernie was thinking of life on his camp, but pregnancy happened surprisingly little there.

'To me, yes.'

'To anybody now.'

She sighed and it was as if the foetus prematurely sighed inside her. The Top Sergeant had seemed so glamorous, looking just like John Garfield, beguilingly dark, permanently tanned and just slightly pudgy, and as soon as he called her 'honey' her legs went all of a wobble. The Forewoman at the R.O.F. had lent them her chalet by Rudyard Lake, perhaps hoping this would happen. And it had been like the time with Malcolm, cooking, boating, strolling the bare-branched woods, catching cold and making love. It had seemed the real thing, so they took no precautions. He promised to take her home when the war was over. She would see Hollywood and New York and forget Malcolm and the backstreets and the smell of explosives. When the sergeant spoke of his home, tears came to his eyes and it was as if he was reciting poetry.

She didn't know what she felt about being pregnant. She had been terrified at first, but now she was back to her usual shrugging humour. She hated the comfy-cat-look that so many girls wore in this state, but she was determined not to go around as if she had world's burden in her belly.

'There's one thing about it.'

They turned back to each other from gazing at the fading horizon.

'What?'

'Me mam's had to stop saying well-trodden soil never fertilises.'

Ernie laughed.

'What does she say then?'

'Nowt. Well, the usual stuff about how I've made me bed and must lie on it. It's me dad who went stark staring mad. At first. But when I threatened to go and put myself in the canal, he got the wind up and now he's all soft and careful. People are funny, honestly.'

He guessed from her eyes, that looked older than the rest of her, what she had been through. It was typical of her to put herself to him in the worst light. It moved him, too, that she was being so familiar with him, as if it was the most natural thing in the world and their old time was restored to them. It seemed he knew who she was again, the strangeness gone. But then her old sharpness flashed up.

'You get a lot of leave, don't you? It was quite lucky really, your gra'ma being ill.'

'What d'you mean?'

'Well, you can't be sent abroad, can you? I mean, to fight. Got a cushy office job, I gather.'

He fixed his eyes on a narrow strip of forgotten ground between the walls of two high workhouse buildings. There was not room to squeeze through and no sunlight managed to shaft in. Yet campion sprouted out of that shade, and dandelions lit it.

'I wanted to join the Medical Corps.'

'Non-combatant?'

'I wanted to go abroad.'

'You know what them medics are, don't you? Lot of ponces, so I'm told.'

'They get killed anyway.'

She nodded and smiled, relenting.

'Coming home for a cuppa?'

He hesitated. Then

'I won't say no.' He smiled back.

XIX

But for the war they might never have bothered with each other. He stayed at her home while he arranged the removal of goods from his own into sale or store. The girl guessed what he, who had always seemed to make a religion of habits and customs, went through as the familiar things were uprooted from their proper places: faded and stained fireside chairs, the solid oak dresser and table, brass candlesticks, hammocky beds, his piano. It seemed that what these things meant to him he meant to her.

One Sunday they went to Selham Park for a picnic. The Hall and half the park were used now for a p.o.w. camp. From time to time they met squads of prisoners marching on the paths, in their loose hopeless green, grinning cockily at the alien world around them or just staring at nothing. Sheila glittered at the glances she got, congratulating herself that she could still make an effect, brassy and pregnant as she was. Ernie tried to smile forgivingly and felt uneasy. The air was scented with pines and rhododendron leaves; the feet, thudding on the brown-needled paths, crunching on the gravel, finally withdrew to wire enclosures and were puppeted about by white-webbed sentries who looked more hostile than the Germans. Quietness came, save for a hoarse shout from beyond a camouflaged cookhouse whose chimney smoked oilily into the blue air.

Ernie and Sheila followed the path into the Italian

Gardens, which were still beautiful, still twined everywhere with the coming roses, still watched over by silver cupolas and stone gods. The foreign prisoners tended this English world, mindless of what it meant. And this little world went on, even though the fountains had stopped playing. Over in the woodland clearing, where the Hordells' cottage used to stand, a concrete clock-tower above an empty swimming-bath told the hours of freedom and captivity. Then there was the Orangery, extended now into a makeshift modern ballroom. Loud-speakers hidden in the trees threaded the western wind with Glenn Miller's *American Patrol*. The old Earl on his hill-top pedestal, seeing and hearing, knew about the deluge. Of the workers, prisoners and servicemen scattered over the careful pattern of his park like jumbled pieces of a forgotten game, perhaps only Ernie knew what *he* knew: what Selham had been.

Sheila grew irritated by her friend's reverie and steered him to a tea-kiosk. When he brought the heavy cups to her where she sat on the grass and fished for a saccarine bottle in her shoulder-bag, she said,

'Well, you're back where you belong now, aren't you?'

'Nobody belongs here now, least of all him.' He jerked his head at the statue. 'My father thought it'd belong to ordinary people one day, and they'd love it and take care of it. But do they? It's messed about any old how. It's a no-man's land.'

'I've often thought I'd like to live out this way. Wouldn't you?'

Ernie did not answer. Sheila smoothed her stained legs thoughtfully.

'Don't you ever think of getting married, Ernie?'

'I did think of it—I even nearly asked Liddy once.

166

But Mr. Cahill got in too quick. There's no point now. Anyway, I'm not the type.'

'Don't be so daft.'

'Well, what about *you*?'

'What d'you mean?'

Her eyes looked sideways, humorously, as she borrowed his pencil to stir her tea.

'I mean, aren't *you* thinking of it?'

He did not mean he was presuming to think of marrying her, and he blushed in case that was what she thought.

'How can I?'

'Your G.I. might come back.'

'He might but he won't.'

Her face looked suddenly drawn and old. Then it lightened.

'But I don't intend getting into me middle age all on me own. I'd even settle for an old man, like Liddy. She's really got her head screwed on has Liddy. Hey, remember what Doris Slater used to say about hubbies?'

They laughed, startling a blackbird who had run head-long at an earwig.

'Ah, but you wouldn't really, though, Sheila, not an old man, would you?'

He couldn't bear the thought.

'Why not? I mean, with a kid I'd be a bit of a liability to a young un.' She patted her belly. The blackbird was watching her from a bush as if interested. 'And anyway, old men are more faithful and loving, you know. Of course, he'd have to be *clean*.'

In their brief silence the bird flew back to its meal. Ernie looked at Sheila's sandals. The stain was streaky on her feet, and he felt so sorry for her he could have cried. It was because the little girl she had been was so near this painted surface.

'You don't mean it, do you?' He veiled his urgency with an odd laugh.

'Of course I do. Most normal women think any man's better than none at all.'

'Any?'

'Well, you know, one you can get on with. I mean, you don't have to be crackers about people——'

'Don't you?'

He stared hot-eyed into the trees where the blackbird invisibly sang. He felt himself as heavy as earth.

Bloody hell, she thought, what have I said? She looked at him, particularly at his trousery thighs. He still wasn't much cop. Somebody could make something of him probably. But not *me*. He wasn't, when all was said and done, *that* repulsive. But not for *me*. His collar-bone was hollowly white at the open neck of his shirt. Perhaps, though, one should make do with what there was and not expect idols to come down to one. Marry a makeshift. Like Liddy.

She could not see how he was palpitating as his eyes ranged over the depths of green as over time, how his mind was, for him, striding like mad through possibilities. The thought of sinking his life into a woman's. Sheila's. He glanced at her. Her hair-roots were not even their old colour let alone blonde. She would never get back to being what she had been. Did he really want to marry her? Somehow it seemed not, now that it might be possible. Is that what she was hinting at any way? Or was it one of her teases?

'Shall we go up Quarry Hill?' he suggested.

They went through the gate behind the Hall and so

into a wilder part of the park, where the deer had once been. Sheila fell behind Ernie's stooping dogged progress. She was irritated with herself for being so easily tired and with him for picking his way so carefully through the buttercups so as not to tread them down. When she got to the top, feeling lathery under her armpits, she found him gazing westward over country that seemed hardly aware of industry or war. He could not tell her that this view always brought the Angel's Allelujah from Elgar's *Gerontius* into his mind. She would not have known what he meant. She nudged him round to face east and the funnelled towns and, pointing to a line of new houses, panted,

'That's where I'd like to live when the war's over,' adding, after a pause, 'Wouldn't you?'

She was daring him to say something definite, but he couldn't. She did not care to hear it but she wanted him to say it. Whatever's up with me, she wondered. He's O.K., the lad is. He's as good as anybody else as far as I can see. But he's not my type at all. Oh God, why isn't he my type? Why do looks matter? She hoped her baby would be a boy and take after his father. She might even love it then. As it was, she was none too keen on kids, and wasn't a bit convinced when people said, 'You'll feel different about your own.'

Why, he was thinking, why, oh why was sex so important? He cleared his throat and she looked expectingly round at him, so he had to say it.

'There's one thing I've learned through this war.'

'What?'

'Sex—you know—that's all there is between a feller and a girl.'

She looked hard at him. Why had he said that?

Now they were sitting astride a thick smooth white log looking at each other, remembering how logs like this had been boats for them once, or zeppelins, only then they had both faced the same way. Ernie always knew he should never have grown up.

'No, you're wrong,' she cried, then lowered her voice as a head was seen jerking towards the brow of the hill. 'It isn't all there is.'

But inside herself she asked, is it?

'And yet you wouldn't have me even if I asked you,' Ernie smiled, trying to make his words as light as swifts who spanned the air before curving straight into their quarry-holes.

His glasses caught the sun as his head jerked to look up into the sparse old windy beech-tops. He could hardly breathe, but to his relief,

'No duck, I wouldn't,' she said, shaking her head and also smiling. 'But that's not all there is either.'